Winn planted a kiss atop Cam's head, his eyes filled with such tenderness it made Hailey want to weep.

She wished all those who called Winn a cold fish could see him now. Gentle, kind and so full of love for a little boy who wasn't even his flesh and blood.

"Good night, sport." Winn pulled up the covers.

When the child's breathing grew even and regular, Winn gently tugged the toy soldier from Cam's hand. He placed the infantryman on top of the nightstand.

Hailey didn't speak until they were back in the living room.

"You're a good father." She could have said more, could have told him there was nothing so sexy as a man who was kind to children. But she felt strangely off-balance.

It was almost as if she and Winn had turned a corner she hadn't known they'd been approaching. Avoiding his gaze, Hailey lifted her bag then slung it over her shoulder.

"There's no reason for you to rush off."

Something in his voice wrapped itself around her spine and caused an inward shudder. The air suddenly hummed with electricity, and Hailey couldn't move. Not if that step took her away from him.

Hoping she wasn't making a huge mistake, she whirled and shot Winn a flirty smile. "Entice me to stay."

* * *

READY, SET, I DO!

BY
CINDY KIRK

MILLS
BOON

Published in Great Britain 2014
by Mills & Boon, an imprint of Harlequin (UK) Limited,
Eton House, 18-24 Paradise Road, Richmond, Surrey, TW9 1SR

© 2014 Cynthia Rutledge

ISBN: 978-0-263-91302-6

23-0714

Harlequin (UK) Limited's policy is to use papers that are natural, renewable and recyclable products and made from wood grown in sustainable forests. The logging and manufacturing processes conform to the legal environmental regulations of the country of origin.

Printed and bound in Spain
by Blackprint CPI, Barcelona

Cindy Kirk has loved to read for as long as she can remember. In first grade she received an award for reading one hundred books. As she grew up, summers were her favorite time of year. Nothing beat going to the library, then coming home and curling up in front of the window air conditioner with a good book. Often the novels she read would spur ideas, and she'd make up her own story (always with a happy ending). When she'd go to bed at night, instead of counting sheep she'd make up more stories in her head. Since selling her first story to Mills & Boon in 1999, Cindy has been forced to juggle her love of reading with her passion for creating stories of her own...but she doesn't mind. Writing for the Mills & Boon® Cherish™ series is a dream come true. She only hopes you have as much fun reading her books as she has writing them!

Cindy invites you to visit her website, www.cindykirk.com.

To my fabulous editor, Patience Bloom.
By the time this book comes out, we'll have
worked together for fifteen years. All I can think is,
how did I get so lucky? Here's to fifteen more!

Chapter One

Hailey Randall sat alone at a table for two in the Hill of Beans coffee shop and brooded about what an idiot she'd been. Discovering her boyfriend had been using her had tumbled her usual sunny mood into stormy, overcast and dark. Hailey pressed her lips together and savagely broke off a piece of scone.

"You're going to have to tone down that dazzling smile."

Hailey glanced up and saw Cassidy Kaye, owner of Jackson Hole's popular Clippety Do Dah Salon, stagger back with one hand shielding her eyes. "It's—it's blinding me."

"Har, har." Even as she spoke, Hailey's lips twitched. "Shouldn't you be hacking off somebody's hair?"

"Your effusive welcome warms my heart. Why, yes, I'd love to join you." Cassidy, dressed in skintight leopard-print leggings and a frilly purple shirt, dropped into the empty seat at the table. Today her bright gold hair was tipped in fuchsia.

"Have a seat," Hailey said, even though her friend was

already sitting, stretching one long leg over the other, a diamond ankle chain winking in the light.

"My ten o'clock canceled. Told me she came down with the stomach flu during the night." The hairstylist shuddered. "Gave me all the gory details."

"Details," Hailey said pointedly, "you will keep to yourself."

Cassidy grinned as she reached over and took a piece of Hailey's cinnamon-chip scone. "I'm thrilled she didn't come in. I can't afford to get sick. Not with Daffy and me doing hair and makeup for the Finster wedding this weekend."

Hailey lifted the latte to her lips. Cass was great with hair, but Hailey had a hard time seeing Daffodil, her waiflike assistant who moved like a closemouthed ghost, doing makeup. "Does Daff even wear makeup?"

"She doesn't need beauty enhancements," Cassidy said matter-of-factly then snagged another piece of scone. She lifted it to her mouth as her eyes narrowed on Hailey's cup. "What kind of latte is that?"

"Cinnamon dulce."

Cassidy gave an exaggerated roll of her eyes. "Cinnamon latte. Cinnamon-chip scone. You've got to shake things up a bit, kiddo. Be bold. Not quite so…predictable."

Though Hailey couldn't exactly see how ordering two favorite items qualified as predictable, she simply smiled. "Trust me. I have my moments."

Cassidy nodded approvingly. "Like giving Josh the boot."

Hailey's smile vanished. She should have realized word would have gotten around by now.

"All I have to say is, about damn time." Cassidy punctuated the announcement with a decisive nod.

Hailey had the feeling that would be most of her friends' response. The few she'd already told about the split had seen Josh for what he was long before she had, which only made her feel even more foolish.

Until two days ago, Hailey had believed Joshua Gratzke had fallen for her and fallen hard. When she bumped into Josh—a former high school classmate—several months ago at the market, he'd made his interest clear. Though they'd never dated way back when, she'd always thought he was cute.

Those days at Jackson Hole High had been almost ten years ago. His face was leaner now, his dark hair shorter, but his smile seemed even more charming. He told her he'd returned to Jackson Hole after law school to consider his options.

With her only working PRN—as needed—at the hospital as a speech therapist, they'd had plenty of time to get reacquainted.

Plenty of time for him to take advantage.

"I didn't see it, Cass." She met the hairstylist's vivid blue eyes. "I foolishly believed he'd fallen head over heels. The fact that he wanted to hang out with my fam was a point in his favor. Sure, we spent extra time with Tripp. He's my brother and we're close. I never thought Josh was angling for a job in Tripp's office."

It still boggled Hailey's mind that her big brother, the one who used to give her noogies, was now the mayor of Jackson Hole, Wyoming.

Cassidy's eyes darkened, as if reliving old memories. "People disappoint us. Even those we think we know well."

"I should have seen the signs," Hailey murmured, almost to herself. "I must have had blinders on."

"Don't be hard on yourself. Josh was smooth." Cassidy reached over and squeezed Hailey's hand. "He almost fooled me."

"*Almost* being the key word."

"Trust me when I say I've had much more experience with slimy men than you." Cassidy's lips lifted in a wry smile. "My internal radar is primed to spot 'em at a hundred paces."

"I won't make the same mistake again." Her appetite gone, Hailey shoved the plate containing the scone in front of Cassidy. She refused to waste one more second on Josh. "Tell me all about Susan Finster's wedding."

"She, or rather her mommy-dearest, insisted on the works." Cassidy leaned back in her chair. "Made it clear if I couldn't do all, she'd take her business elsewhere."

"If you end up needing help, let me know." Hailey forced a casual tone, not wanting to put her friend on the spot but determined to make her interest clear. "I used to work as a cosmetics consultant in college and really enjoyed it."

Cassidy dropped the scone to the plate, leaned forward. The gaze that pinned Hailey had a predatory gleam. "Seriously?"

"Everyone said I had the knack."

"No, I mean, are you serious about helping?"

"Totally." Hailey found herself pleased by Cassidy's reaction. "I'd love to help."

"I cannot friggin' believe it." Cassidy bopped herself in the head with the heel of one hand. "I've been beating my brains out for weeks trying to think of someone and here, you've been right under my nose."

"Glad to know I'm not the only one who misses the obvious."

Hailey's dry tone brought a smile to Cassidy's lips. The hairstylist straightened in her seat and leaned forward. "I want us to work together, Hailey."

"Talk about ordering a cake before you know if the flavor suits you." Hailey kept her tone light even as her heart started to rev. "You don't know if I have talent."

"One look at you tells me you're great with makeup." Cassidy waved away Hailey's concern using a hand tipped with royal-blue nails. Those who didn't know her well often dismissed the salon owner as the crazy artistic type. But ten minutes with her was all it took to know this was a savvy businesswoman, determined to grow her already thriving business. "I've had clients come in with suggestions you've given them about their hair and you've been spot on, especially with color."

Hailey flushed with pleasure. It was true her friends often asked her opinion on what they should do with their hair. "You really want me to work for you?"

"No, not really." Cassidy studied her thoughtfully. Tapped a long fingernail against her bright pink lips.

"*With* me," Cassidy clarified. "A partnership."

Blood coursed through Hailey's veins. She saw herself working with clients, offering advice and instruction on makeup and hairstyling changes that would enhance a woman's natural beauty. She wanted to seize this opportunity and run with it. But she made herself slow down. Josh had taught her that if something seemed too good to be true, it was best to take a step back. "Why a partnership?"

"You need to think of this venture as yours. I want you to use your social connections to help this new business fly."

The chill that swept through Hailey cut deep, all the way to the bone. "I thought you wanted my expertise, but all—"

"Don't get on your high horse." Cassidy gave a dismissive wave. "This is a new venture. I'll be bringing my years in business, my license and *my* connections to the table. You'd be providing a keen eye, your experience with cosmetics and *your* connections."

Hailey tamped down her anger and focused on the facts. After a couple of seconds, she let out a breath and nodded. "I guess that makes sense."

"Certainly does." Cassidy pushed back her chair. She stood there for a moment, a curvaceous woman who commanded attention. "We can discuss particulars when you've decided you're interested."

"Don't you mean *if* I decide I'm interested?"

"We're both champing at the bit to get this thing rolling." Cassidy grinned. "It's just I already know it. You have to think it through before you realize I've dropped a sweet deal right in your lap."

The bell over the door jingled and Winston Ferris strolled into the shop, cell phone to his ear. Hailey's heart skipped a beat at the sight of her good-looking neighbor.

Tall, with an athletic build, Winn had the confident demeanor of a person used to giving orders. His dark hair was cut stylishly short and though his handsome face would draw any woman's attention, it was his steely hazel eyes that defined him.

"I need to get back to the salon." Cassidy gestured with her head toward Winn. "I'll leave you to canoodle with your new boyfriend."

Hailey pulled her brows together. "Winn is my neighbor not my boyfriend."

Cassidy merely gave a wink and strolled away, a broad smile on her pouty pink lips.

"It's a setback, nothing more." Winn absolutely refused to let his emotions show on his face as he listened to his boss's rant. He prided himself on his self-control, even if it wasn't always easy. He gave a short nod of acknowledgment to Cassidy Kaye as the business owner strolled past him on her way out the door, a flamboyant leopard with pink hair and a hot body.

His boss finally ran out of air and abruptly disconnected. Winn pocketed the phone. It was never easy telling a man accustomed to getting his way that the golf-course development they'd spent months trying to get approved had hit another snag. The final vote on the project was delayed. Again.

Forget the coffee, Winn thought. A stiff shot of whiskey would better suit his mood.

But when he saw Cole Lassiter standing behind the counter, Winn changed his mind. Cole was a driving force in Jackson Hole and walking out of his shop once he'd been seen wouldn't be a smart move. Winn was all about smart moves.

"Cole." Winn offered a smile to the man behind the Hill of Beans coffee-shop empire. "What's the head honcho doing working the counter?"

"Learning the challenges my people face," Cole said easily. "I work each position periodically. Since this store is in the town where I live, it's easy to do here."

Anyone seeing Cole, with his shaggy dark hair and green apron over casual shirt and jeans, would never peg him for a successful entrepreneur. Unless they looked in his eyes and saw the sharp gleam of intelligence and a hint of a take-no-prisoners brawler beneath the civilized facade.

"Makes sense." Winn lifted the briefcase. "I thought I'd grab a cup of caffeine and look over some reports."

"Just coffee then?"

"Black and strong."

"Coming right up." Cole turned toward the stainless-steel machine.

Winn used the moment to glance around the shop. To his way of thinking, networking was a 24/7 thing. Unfortunately, with ten o'clock being right between the morning crowd and lunch rush, the place was fairly quiet.

His gaze had almost made it around the dining area when it locked on the petite blue-eyed blonde dressed casually in jeans and a hot-pink hoodie. The sight of her made him smile.

Hailey Randall. His next-door neighbor. Alone.

Winn had been hoping to speak with her for days. Though he told himself—again—that her personal life was none of his concern, once he got his coffee, he headed straight across the dining area to her table.

She looked up from her phone as he approached, her welcoming smile bringing an unexpected shot of light to his day.

"May I join you?" he asked politely.

She gestured to the empty chair. "Please do."

"I didn't expect to see you here this morning."

"Ditto," she said with an impish grin, relaxing against the back of her chair. "I haven't seen you around lately. Were you out of town again?"

Winn took a sip of his coffee before answering, and was impressed by the rich, robust flavor. No wonder Hill of Beans was so successful.

"I was helping put up hay at my dad's ranch." Winn took another long drink and felt some of his tension ease.

"That's hard work." A doubtful look crossed Hailey's pretty face. "You don't seem like the physical-labor type to me."

"I don't know whether I should be insulted or flattered." Winn chuckled. "The truth is, I enjoy getting hot and sweaty as much as the next guy."

There'd been no intent to be suggestive, but for a second there was…something in the air. A spark, an awareness that he'd experienced before but had ignored. After all, Hailey was not only seven years younger than he, she was his neighbor. More important, he considered her a friend. One of the few he had in Jackson Hole.

That was why he had to be honest with her. Though he realized Hailey and Josh had only been dating steadily a couple of months, the guy was another Vanessa.

He'd tried to tell himself her jerk of a boyfriend was none of his business and to just let it go. Then he would think of Vanessa, a woman he'd dated for almost a year. A woman he thought he might love. A woman he trusted, who'd slept with another man when they were supposedly in a monogamous relationship.

Winn wished someone had told him the score. Hard as it would have been to hear, it would have saved him a lot of grief.

"I have something to tell you."

"If you're going to say you're quitting the business world to be a rodeo clown, give me a sec to order a double shot of espresso," she said with a teasing smile. "After the putting-up-hay revelation, I can't take another shock. Not without a hefty dose of caffeine."

Winn laughed and shook his head. From day one, Hailey had enchanted him. How could anyone not be charmed by this woman, with her winning smile and sunny personality? That was why he'd put off the task he now faced. The last thing he wanted was to bring her pain. "It's not about me. It's about Josh."

The man's name tasted foul on his tongue.

Her smile wavered, just a little. When she picked up her cup and took a sip, her hand trembled, as well. "What about him?"

"He's not the man you think he is—"

"Oh, Winn." Her laugh sounded brittle, like a fragile egg ready to shatter into a million pieces. "I think I know him pretty well by now."

It only figured she wasn't going to make this easy. He'd start with the basics and save the best—or rather the worst—for the finale.

"The man can't be trusted, Hailey. He's out for himself."

To his surprise, Hailey looked slightly amused. "Is the pot calling the kettle black?"

Winn blinked. "What?"

"You and your father are masters at looking out for number one." There wasn't an ounce of censure in Hailey's matter-of-fact tone. "It only figures you'd recognize those characteristics in Josh."

What was he supposed to say to that? Did she even expect a response?

"You're aware of Josh's duplicity?" Winn spoke slowly, cautiously, feeling like a soldier making his way through a minefield.

"I am." Though her tone gave nothing away, her eyes took on a sheen.

Winn's gut clenched. Josh was a rotten little weasel for putting that look in her eyes. "How did you find out?"

Her strangled laugh told him she was close to letting those tears fall. "You mean, how did I finally wise up to the fact he was using me to get close to my brother?"

Now Winn was thoroughly confused. "I was talking about the woman he's been dating in Idaho Falls."

Hailey dropped her cup to the table with a clatter. But when she spoke, her voice was deadly calm. "What woman?"

"An attorney named Kelly. That's all I know." He paused as her earlier words sank in. "He was using you to get close to Tripp? Why?"

Before answering, she scrubbed her hands across her face. When she met his gaze, her eyes were dry.

"Apparently, Josh has political aspirations. Tripp is considering hiring a mayoral assistant." She lifted the latte to her lips but only held it there. "What better way to get a leg up on the competition than to become personally acquainted with the man himself through his beloved little sister?"

Winn heard the pain beneath the sarcasm. Though he might admire Josh's ability to think outside the box in pursuit of a goal, he decried his ethics. "How did you find out?"

"A friend of a friend." Hailey raised one shoulder in a slight shrug. "He'd done some bragging. It got back to me."

"He's a fool."

"*I* was the fool." Hailey's chuckle held no humor. "Up to now, I consoled myself with the fact that he liked me, at least a little. Now it appears I was truly only a means to an end. Tell me how you found out about the attorney."

Winn hated the sadness that darkened her eyes. "She doesn't matter."

"I want to know." Hailey reached across the table, clamped her fingers around his wrist. "Tell me."

He looked into those baby blues and his heart wrenched. What he told her would only add to her pain and he was sorry for it.

"Last week I had a lunch meeting in Idaho Falls," he began.

With a metro population well over a hundred thousand, Winn hadn't expected to run into anyone he knew. Then, across the dining room at a trendy eatery on A Street, he'd spotted Josh with a pretty brunette.

He assumed it was strictly business between the two... until he saw them kiss. It wasn't a little peck, either. Winn's associate had noticed him staring and mentioned Kelly was an attorney at his wife's legal firm. The guy with her was her boyfriend, Josh.

By the time Winn finished, Hailey's face had gone stony.

She pressed her lips together. "A cheat as well as an opportunist."

Winn took a sip of coffee and nodded.

"I don't appreciate being played for a fool."

"Who does?" Winn understood the sense of shock, betrayal and embarrassment. Even after almost eight years, the fact that he'd been played so completely still stuck in his craw.

"Thanks for telling me. I appreciate it." Hailey's lips lifted in a tremulous smile. "Some wouldn't have said a word."

"The way I see it, if you can't trust your friends to have your back, what good are they?" Winn said casually.

But when he met her gaze, he had to fight back the sudden urge to take her in his arms, to kiss her until the sadness had vanished from her eyes and the sunny smile was back on her lips.

Friends, he thought with a rueful smile. *Yeah, right.*

Chapter Two

After the discussion with his boss and subsequent conversation with Hailey, the last person Winn wanted to see was his father. But he promised his dad he'd stop by the ranch at noon. And that, he thought sourly, gave credence to the saying that bad things came in threes.

Winn turned off the highway onto a long lane with white fences on each side. He mentally put his Mercedes on autopilot and considered how much to divulge about his recent setback. While he might now be playing gentleman rancher, Jim Ferris was a businessman to the core. In his father's eyes, if a man failed at anything it was his own damn fault. That was exactly how he'd view the project delay.

Though the golf-course development remained a political hot potato because of the environmentally sensitive guidelines it butted up against, the delay was on Winn's back. He should have found palms to grease or, failing that, pushed harder. As his father was fond of saying, only a fool takes no for an answer.

Winn pulled his car to a stop in front of the sprawling ranch home and decided he'd answer his father's questions honestly but not bring up the matter first. Barely noticing the beds of flowers in full bloom flanking the walkway, Winn stepped to the front door and knocked.

He'd been told many times there was no need for such formality, but walking unannounced into a home that wasn't his didn't feel right.

After a few moments, Elena Hernandez, his father's housekeeper, opened the door with a welcoming smile. Though she was close to his dad's age, the jet-black hair pulled back in a twist didn't show the slightest hint of gray. Today, she wore dark tailored pants and a crisp white shirt.

Winn wondered if the outfit was her idea or his father's. Regardless, she must not have an issue with the new uniform. From what Winn observed, Elena had a way of getting her way without the old man realizing it. That talent alone made Winn admire and respect her.

"It's nice to see you, Mr. Ferris."

"Good morning—ah—afternoon, Elena." Winn glanced around the entryway with its beamed ceilings and travertine, stucco walls.

Normally by this time his father would be bellowing how he was late, even if Winn was early. But the house stood quiet, with only the soft swish from a ceiling fan and a faint, sultry salsa beat that appeared to be coming from the kitchen.

Winn lifted a brow and Elena flushed. "Mr. Ferris did not mention he was expecting visitors."

"This place needs a little music."

Relief washed over Elena's face.

"Is he in his office?"

"I'm afraid your father isn't here."

The meeting time had only been set last night. Winn pulled his brows together. "Where is he?"

"In Idaho Falls, I believe. A business meeting."

Winn fought a stab of temper. The old man could have at least called or texted the change in plans.

"The meeting was last-minute," Elena confided. "A red-hot deal."

Winn couldn't help it. The wry amusement in her eyes when she drawled the words made him laugh.

"May I offer you lunch?"

"No, I—"

"I made chicken escabeche."

The look in Elena's eyes told him she'd filed the fact that the cold Mediterranean salad was one of his favorites from the time he'd lived at the ranch.

When Winn had first arrived in Jackson Hole, he'd planned to stay only a few weeks. Living at the ranch seemed to make sense. It hadn't taken Winn long to realize he and his dad did better with lots of distance between them.

"Mr. Ferris?" Elena waited with a smile on her lips.

"I'm definitely staying for lunch."

Elena started out of the room then paused in the doorway." Would you prefer to eat in the dining room or on the terrace?"

"The terrace." Winn pulled his phone from his pocket. "I'd like a glass of iced tea, too, please."

"Yes, sir. Right away."

Winn made his way to the flagstone terrace shaded by tall, leafy trees. He chose one of the comfortable chairs positioned strategically around a counter-high fire pit.

While he waited for his lunch, Winn made quick calls to city hall and let several high-placed officials know just how unhappy he was with the latest round of delays.

He turned at the sound of the French doors opening. Elena stepped out with a cut-crystal glass filled with ice and what he hoped was unsweetened tea.

"Lots of ice, just as you like." The housekeeper placed

the glass on the side table next to his chair. "Your lunch will be right out."

"No rush." Winn lifted the hand holding the phone. "I have calls to return."

"You and your father." Elena clucked her tongue. "Always working."

"What else is there?" he said automatically.

Elena opened her mouth then closed it and only smiled.

It was obvious she didn't understand the drive he and his father shared. But then, not many did. Elena probably thought his emphasis should be on home and family rather than business. But that road could be a rocky one.

He thought of the look in Hailey's eyes when he told her he'd seen Josh with another woman. And the unmistakable pain on her face when she relayed how the creep had been using her to get close to Tripp.

He thought of Vanessa, a woman he once thought he might love. She was a kindergarten teacher with a girl-next-door persona and zest for life. In some ways, she reminded him of Hailey. But just as Hailey had discovered that Josh couldn't be trusted, he'd learned the bubbly Vanessa was a liar and a cheat.

Winn raked his hand through his hair, forcing air past the sudden tightness in his chest. He hated that Josh's cheating on Hailey had caused him to think about Vanessa and her fiancé. He preferred to keep thoughts of that time in the back of his mind, locked tight in a rarely opened file cabinet.

Winn heard the doorbell chime and straightened. It appeared he wasn't the only visitor his father stood up today.

"Come in, Miss Hailey." Elena's voice radiated welcome. The women spoke in lowered tones for several seconds. Other than the initial greeting, *he's in the barn* were the only words Winn made out.

Curious as to who was the mysterious "he" Hailey had come to see, Winn pulled to his feet.

He reached the foyer and found Elena trying to convince the pretty blonde, still wearing the hot-pink hoodie, to stay for lunch.

"Thanks for the offer," Hailey told the housekeeper, "but my parents are expecting me and—"

Hailey's eyes widened when she saw him. "Winn. I didn't realize you were here."

He smiled quizzically. "My car is parked out front. Didn't you see it?"

"I saw a sedan in the driveway. I thought it was your father's."

Winn winced. He loved the S550, but was going to have to see about exchanging it for a sportier model. Driving an old man's car didn't fit the image he wanted to project. After putting a new vehicle on his mental list for tomorrow, Winn refocused on Hailey.

"Reconsider Elena's offer and join me for lunch," he said with an easy smile, leaning against the doorjamb. "Did she mention we're having chicken escabeche? I bet she could also scare up a glass of sangria for you."

"I don't think—"

"Don't tell me you're full," Winn said. "The scone you had this morning can't be enough to hold you."

Winn ignored the gleam of speculation in Elena's eyes. He *could* explain he and Hailey had shared coffee at Hill of Beans, but that was their business. Taking Hailey's arm, Winn made an executive decision. He turned to Elena. "Miss Randall will join me for lunch on the terrace."

"Yes, sir." Elena hurried off, ignoring Hailey's faint murmur of protest.

Two bright swaths of pink colored Hailey's cheeks. "I didn't come over expecting to be fed."

"You made Elena happy." Winn kept his tone conversational as he took her arm and ushered her through the house to the terrace. "Now, tell me about this man hidden in the barn."

"Man?" Hailey stopped dead in her tracks, a frown furrowing her pretty brow. "What man?"

"Elena told you he was in the barn."

Hailey dropped into a chair. The peel of laughter that burst from her lips both puzzled and delighted him. Try as he might to fight it, the gregariousness of the woman seated across the table had always appealed to him.

"The *he* is a dog."

Winn blinked.

"Barks. Four legs." Hailey's tone was serious, though she appeared to be struggling not to laugh again.

Elena appeared with a glass of sangria and a tray of tapas, including mixed olives and cheese. The housekeeper's smile appeared to widen at the ease between him and Hailey. Elena slipped back into the house to finish the salad preparation with a light step.

"The dog is a stray." Hailey took a sip of sangria. Pleasure sparked in her blue eyes. "This is good. Try it."

She thrust out the sangria. Winn obligingly drank and wondered what it'd be like if, instead of the glass, his lips closed over hers? Would her mouth taste as sweet as the sangria?

Winn shoved the thought aside and handed the fruity drink back with an easy smile. "Very nice."

When she placed her lips on the glass, Winn experienced a hard punch of lust. It wasn't the first time he'd felt this, but she was his neighbor and just coming off a difficult breakup. He leaned back in his chair and forced a composure he didn't feel. "Tell me about the animal you came to see."

He listened as she explained the border collie mix had strayed onto his father's property. No one had reported the dog missing. Apparently it had been hanging around for several weeks. The ranch hands hadn't let him starve.

"The shelter said, based on the information given, he'd probably been dumped."

"You came all the way out here just to catch a look at some stray?"

"His name is Bandit." Hailey spoke almost primly. "It was engraved on a tag hooked to his collar."

"Makes sense." Winn lifted his glass of tea and frowned slightly. "I guess."

"When the dog was found, your father told Bobby to take him immediately to the shelter, but Bobby—and some of the other guys—wanted to try to find him a new home. The shelter was full and there was a chance he'd be put down. From what I gather, he's a smart, sweet boy, young though, more puppy than—"

Winn held up a hand, like a schoolboy waiting for the teacher to call on him.

Hailey smiled. "Yes, Winn."

"Who's Bobby?"

"One of your father's ranch hands." Her tone implied it was something he should have known. "Bobby and I went to high school together."

"So a friend from high school—who now works for my father—called you."

"Actually, I ran into Bobby downtown. He told me about Bandit."

"The border collie."

"A+, Winn." She unexpectedly grinned. "You're paying attention."

"One major piece of the puzzle doesn't fit. Why would someone put a dog's name on a tag but not their contact information?"

Hailey lifted her shoulders in a little shrug. "Why would someone dump a dog?"

"I'm surprised your friend didn't take him." Winn grimaced. He wasn't into wasting time. So why was he having a conversation about a stray?

"Bobby's place doesn't allow pets." Hailey paused to savor another sip of sangria. "I've been thinking about getting a dog, so I said I'd take a look. If I like what I see, I'll take him home."

Yep, he really was wasting time discussing a dog. Winn opened his mouth, determined to change the subject, when Hailey lowered her voice to a conspiratorial whisper.

"Bobby told me I could take *him* home, too." She chuckled. "A two-for-one deal."

An uncomfortable tightness gripped his gut, but Winn reminded himself it wasn't any of his business who she dated...or took home to her bed. "Are you taking him up on the offer?"

She rolled her eyes, waved a dismissive hand. "Bobby has a girlfriend. Besides, after that fiasco with Josh, I'm not feeling particularly charitable toward old high-school classmates."

"A+ for you," Winn said, and made her laugh just as Elena appeared with their salads.

"Thanks." Hailey offered the woman an extrawarm smile. "This looks delicious."

"Yes," Winn added. "Much appreciated."

"The woman is a saint," Hailey confided once Elena was out of earshot. "I don't know how she stands—"

She stopped, as if suddenly realizing she was speaking to the son of the man she was about to disparage.

"Don't stop on my account." Winn offered a humorless chuckle. "I'd be the first to acknowledge my father is a difficult and complex man."

That was all he'd say on the matter. As tired as he was of the dog talk, he wanted to discuss his father even less.

Hailey took another big gulp of sangria. "I love dogs, don't you?"

On second thought, perhaps discussing his father wasn't such a bad idea. "I haven't had much contact with animals."

Hailey set down her glass, tilted her head. "Surely you had a dog growing up?"

"You've met my father. You know how particular he is

about his home, his possessions. Does he appear to be the type of man who'd tolerate a slobbering, hair-shedding, shoe-chewing creature in his home?"

Hailey put a finger to her lips, drawing his attention to her full sensual mouth. "You're right. Definitely not a dog person."

"From what I've observed, a pet of any kind is a big responsibility." Winn placed the linen napkin on his lap with a preciseness that was as much a part of him as his hundred-dollar haircut. "Are you certain you have time for an animal?"

"Absolutely. With Josh out of the picture, my social life is officially nonexistent." Hailey gave a humorless laugh. "I have a great deal of free time. And I get lonely. Don't you?"

"Not really." As a child he'd often been alone, felt alone even when he'd been in a group, but that had been long ago. Now he simply valued his privacy and liked being able to keep everything in its place. With sudden horror, he realized he was very much like his father in that regard.

"After we finish eating, you can come and check out Bandit with me."

Winn started to shake his head, until she took his hand in a friendly, companionable gesture.

"Please, Winn. If I take him home, Bandit will be your neighbor." She squeezed his hand. "I really want your opinion."

Her flesh was warm against his skin and Winn had to resist the urge to curve his fingers around hers.

"I'll give you whatever you want." His tone came out husky with a suggestive undertone.

Their eyes met and held for a long moment.

The sudden twitch of her lips broke the mood. She expelled a little giggle. "For now, I'll settle for your opinion… though I'll reserve the right to ask for more."

Before he could respond, Elena returned briefly with another glass of sangria and a refill of tea.

Hailey smiled warmly at Elena, raving about the salad.

Winn listened with half an ear. He couldn't help wondering what Hailey's version of "more" would involve. Not that it mattered. All Winn knew was if he did get involved with someone in Jackson Hole, it wouldn't be with a woman who reminded him of his greatest mistake.

Hailey crouched and petted the black-and-white dog that thumped his fluffy tail on the ground while licking her outstretched hand. She glanced up at Winn. "Isn't he the cutest thing ever?"

It was just the two of them in the barn. When Bobby recognized him as Jim's son, he handed Hailey the leash and hurried off.

Winn continued to keep his distance. Though he had no personal experience with dogs, he'd heard they liked leather. His shiny Ferragamo loafers were not meant for the inside of a dog's mouth. Not only that, he could practically see the hair falling from the animal as Hailey rubbed his back.

Winn took another step away. The last thing Winn needed was to show up for his afternoon meeting with dog hair all over his suit. "He appears to be molting."

Hailey laughed, a pleasant sound reminding him of the soft ringing of bells. "The days are getting warmer. His thick coat kept him comfy all winter. Now he's shedding some of his hair for the summer months."

Didn't she realize if she took the animal home, he'd be dropping that hair all over her condo? Winn shuddered at the thought. *Not in my home,* he thought. *Not in a million years.*

"Do you want to come home with me, Bandito?" Hailey crooned and the dog let out a little whine. "Will you come home with me and be my boy?"

At those words, the molting bundle of fur and slobber leaped up and emitted a series of sharp staccato barks.

Hailey looked up at Winn and grinned. "I knew it. Bandit and me, we're a perfect match."

She looked so pretty and so pleased with herself that Winn was tempted to step closer and pull her into his arms. Instead, he shifted his attention to the dog. "You're going to take him?"

"Absolutely." She clipped the leash on the dog's collar and straightened. "I'd best get him out of here before your father returns."

"Isn't he the one who wanted the dog gone?" Winn's confusion resurfaced. "I think he'd be ecstatic you're taking him."

"The dog was supposed to be gone long ago. Bobby thought he had a home for him, but the person backed out. The only option was the pound and Bobby couldn't bring himself to take Bandit there."

Winn thought of his father. Of the man's exacting standards. His zero tolerance for disobedience.

"You're right. My father would be upset the dog is still here. When he gives orders, he expects them to be followed."

He was helping Hailey load the dog crate into her SUV when his phone rang. He slipped it from his pocket and checked the readout. It was an Atlanta area code but a number he didn't recognize. "Do you mind if I take this?"

Hailey glanced up from where she stood soothing Bandit in the transportation crate. "Not at all. I need to get going any—"

"Don't leave," he said, then answered the call. "Winn Ferris."

"Mr. Ferris. This is Charles Keating with Keating, Exeter and York. We're a law firm in Atlanta and we're handling Ms. Vanessa Abbott's estate. You have—"

As Winn listened to the attorney talk, bile rose inside his throat and an icy chill enveloped him. He forced himself to breathe.

When Mr. Keating paused, Winn cleared his throat and located his voice. He asked questions and received answers but it all seemed surreal. The call ended with Winn promising to take the first flight to Georgia.

"Winn. Is something wrong?"

Even Hailey's warm touch on his arm couldn't begin to reach the chill.

"I have to leave for Atlanta right away." He met her worried gaze. "I need to pick up my son."

Chapter Three

Fried chicken on the stove and garlic-cheese biscuits rising in the oven filled the large country kitchen with delicious aromas. For as long as Hailey could remember, cooking had been one of her mother's passions. And the woman was a master.

Kathy Randall motioned for her daughter to add more milk to the potatoes she was whipping. In her late fifties with dark blond hair cut in a stylish bob, blue eyes and a perpetual twinkle in her eyes, Hailey's mother loved life and it showed. "Are you telling me Winn Ferris has a son?"

"So he said." Hailey frowned and resumed chopping broccoli for the salad. Though there was no reason Winn had to tell all, she fought back a twinge of irritation. "It's kind of a big secret to keep."

"Does he have a wife to go with the son?" There was a hint of disapproval in Kathy's voice. No doubt she was recalling the various single women the business executive had dated since arriving in Jackson Hole.

"The boy's mother, the woman who died in the boating accident, was Winn's former girlfriend. The guy who died with her was her fiancé. Apparently they were planning to be married next month."

"How sad." Kathy gave a sigh of empathy. "Was the child with them when the boat exploded?"

"No. He was playing at a neighbor's."

"Lucky for the boy. If you can call any child who loses his mother lucky." Kathy shifted her gaze to Hailey. "Dying before you and Tripp were grown was my worst fear. I knew your father would do his best, but I believed you needed me."

"I did need you." Hailey gave her mom a quick hug. "I still do. Who else will teach me how to cook?"

Her mother laughed. "I think of all those years I tried. You simply weren't interested."

"It's moved into the priority range now," Hailey told her mom, completely serious. "Unless I want to survive on takeout or soup and sandwiches every night, I have to learn."

"Well, I'm happy to further your educa—"

The backdoor slid open and her father stepped inside, the border collic at his side. "Is it time to eat?"

Frank Randall was a tall man with a rangy body and thick salt-and-pepper hair. Naturally thin, he'd regained the weight he'd lost last year during his successful battle with melanoma.

"Just about," his wife said. "Hailey was telling me that Winn Ferris—"

Hailey's phone rang as her mother was explaining the situation to her father. She glanced down. "It's Winn."

Her father inclined his head. "Why is he calling you?"

"I'm about to find out." Hailey walked from the kitchen into the great room, where the warm earth-toned walls complemented the soaring beamed ceilings in muted white. "Hi, Winn. How are you?"

"Fine." His voice was low and tightly controlled. "We're in Denver now and should land in Jackson at about eight. Cam refuses to eat, but I need to get something into him. Do you remember the chicken noodle soup you made last week?"

"Of course." The soup had been her first foray into making homemade noodles. In a neighborly gesture, she'd taken some to Winn as well as Mrs. Samuelson, who lived on the other side of her.

"Do you have any left?"

Winn's question broke through Hailey's thoughts. While she'd eaten or given away the last of it, she knew her mother had some in her freezer. "As a matter of fact, I do."

"Thanks, Hailey."

The hint of weariness in Winn's voice tugged at her. Though she didn't know all the particulars, she figured his stress level was sky-high.

"It'll be okay, Winn," she said in a low soothing tone. "It will all be okay."

After enjoying a meal with her family, Hailey returned home with a half gallon of her mother's chicken noodle soup and a loaf of homemade oatmeal bread. Winn would never know that this was her mother's soup instead of her own. Although he might think it was even better the second time around.

While the airport wasn't far from their condos, if his plane landed at eight, it would be a while before Winn got home. Hailey used the time to take Bandit for a walk, then began brushing him, while keeping her ear cocked for the sound of Winn's car.

It was almost nine when she heard his garage door slide up. Rather than jumping to her feet and rushing to the door, Hailey waited, knowing Winn would call once he and the boy were settled.

He'd told her Cameron was eight. A lot of her brother's

friends—her friends as well, she reminded herself—had children close to that age. When Hailey had practiced full-time as a speech pathologist in Denver, she'd worked with many children. She liked kids, got along with them, hoped to have a couple of them herself one day.

Idly, she wondered what Winn was like as a father. He'd always been so focused on his business interests that it was hard to imagine him devoting time to anyone or anything else.

Of course, Winn *had* dropped what he was doing to get his son and bring him to Jackson Hole. Her hand stroked the top of Bandit's head and the dog emitted what sounded like a moan of pleasure.

Taking care of a pet had been more work than she'd imagined. If she was Winn and facing the total care of a little boy, she'd be freaking. Other than asking for her help with dinner, Winn had sounded composed and as self-assured as ever on the phone. Yet, something told her he'd sound that way even if he was on the deck of the *Titanic* as it was sinking. From what she'd observed, Winn kept his feelings close.

Tired of sitting, she put the brush aside and rose. Moving to the refrigerator, she peered inside for something to eat. She'd finally decided on a carton of yogurt when her phone buzzed. Hailey smiled as Winn's name flashed on the screen. "You two ready to chow?"

"We are. Or at least I am." Winn hesitated. "Hailey, about Cam—"

Though he couldn't see her, she found herself cocking her head. "What about him?"

"He…" Winn paused. "Nothing. We'll be here whenever it works for you to come over."

The call ended and Hailey stood staring at the phone, her brows knitted. Something was definitely up. She shoved the yogurt back into the refrigerator and hurriedly grabbed the container of soup and the loaf of bread instead. With curiosity fueling her steps, Hailey headed next door.

Winn tried not to stare at the little boy sitting silently on the sofa, hands folded in his lap. Cam still had the same shock of brown hair and hazel eyes that tended toward green, the same skinny frame and big feet. But that was where the resemblance to the son he'd known and loved ended.

This child was pale, with freckles that stood out like shiny pennies across the bridge of his nose. There was no laughter in his eyes, no mischievous glint, just...emptiness and sorrow.

The boy had just lost someone dear to him, Winn reminded himself. Regardless of her actions toward him, Vanessa had been a kind and loving mother. When she'd cast Winn from her life, his one consolation was that Cam would never lack for love. He hadn't known Brandon, other than to despise the man's deliberate attempts to keep him away from Cam.

The boy might have been Brandon's child by blood, but Winn had raised him for the first six years of his life. Now, Brandon and Vanessa were dead. And Winn was Cam's legal guardian.

It was only natural the boy would seem different. Of course, he'd be standoffish and silent. Not only had he lost his parents, he'd been snatched by a man he thought had deserted him and relocated far from the only home he'd known.

"My neighbor, Hailey, is bringing over soup." Winn tried for cheery but couldn't quite pull it off. "It's good stuff. You've got to be hungry. You barely ate today."

On their way to the airport, Winn had stopped at a place that specialized in chicken fingers. He remembered the popular chain as being one of Cam's favorites. The boy had taken only a few bites, then stared out the window.

Although Winn had talked so much that he was sick of the sound of his own voice, Cam had barely uttered five words. All single responses in a barely audible tone.

What had Vanessa done to him? What had that jerk Brandon done to him? Winn tried to contain his rising anger at whatever had brought this change in the boy. While he realized some of what Cam was showing was grief, there was more going on here. He would get to the bottom of it, eventually.

Relief flooded him at the knock on the door.

"That'll be my neighbor." He opened the door and realized she hadn't come alone. The border collie stood beside her, brown eyes staring at him, as if daring Winn to keep him out.

"Bandit wanted to meet Cam." Hailey handed Winn the soup container and breezed past him into the large living room. She wore jeans and a Western-cut shirt in shocking blue. "I hope you don't mind."

The words of protest that had formed on Winn's lips died at the look of surprised pleasure in Cameron's eyes. "Ah, not at all."

"Hi, Cameron." Hailey crossed the room to sit beside the boy on the sofa. She extended her hand. "I'm Hailey Randall. I live next door. Welcome to Jackson Hole."

For a long moment the hand hovered there. Until the boy took it.

"Can you tell Miss Hailey you're pleased to meet her?" Winn gently urged.

"P-p-p-pleased to m-m-mcet you," Cam stuttered.

Hailey's smile never wavered. "I brought you homemade chicken noodle soup. I realize it's late for dinner, but I wasn't in the mood to eat earlier. I'm sure hungry now."

Cam glanced down at his bright neon-green-and-purple sneakers.

"If your dad has a large bowl," Hailey continued without missing a beat, "we could heat the soup in the micro-wave. I'd love for you to try it and tell me if it's any good."

The boy didn't comment but gestured with his head to-ward Bandit, who sat at Hailey's feet. "Who—who is she?"

If Hailey noticed the boy's stuttering—and it would have been impossible not to—it didn't show.

"Bandit. He's a boy," Hailey confided with an easy smile. "Which means I'm outnumbered three to one."

To illustrate her point, she gestured with one hand to-ward Winn, then Cam and finally on Bandit.

The boy's quick flash of a smile loosened the tightness that had held Winn's chest in a stranglehold since he'd re-ceived the call from the attorney.

"Perhaps after we eat," Hailey moved to the cupboards, "we can take Bandit for a short walk. Unless you're too tired."

Cam gestured toward the dog. "C-can we g-go now?"

"I'd really like to eat first," Hailey said, her hands busy. "But you can hold Bandit's leash when we do go, if you'd like."

The boy gave a jerky nod of agreement.

Winn moved to the cupboards and took out bowls and glasses. Hailey put the soup in the microwave while Winn sliced the bread and Cam placed silverware on the table.

At the table, Cameron said nothing. He shoveled in food and kept his eyes on Bandit. Winn wasn't sure if the boy ate because he was hungry or because he wanted to take the dog for a walk.

Once they finished and cleared the dishes, Hailey clipped a leash on Bandit's collar then handed it to Cam. "How about you walk him around inside first? That way you can get a feel for it."

Cam's eyes were wide and serious.

Hailey smiled. "Perhaps you could start by showing him your room."

The boy nodded and the two disappeared down the hallway.

"Thank you." Winn kept his voice low.

Hailey cocked her head. "A few minutes in the microwave is no big deal."

"Thank you for the soup and bread." He gestured toward the hall. "And for being nice to him."

"Normally, I like to be mean to children and small animals, but I thought I'd make an exception tonight."

Winn couldn't help chuckling. But he quickly sobered. "He's not the same boy I left behind in Atlanta two years ago."

"Surely that's not the last time you saw him."

A muscle in Winn's jaw jumped. "Actually it is. He never stuttered before. Do you think—"

He cut off when he heard the sound of the boy and dog coming down the hall. "I'd like to speak to you about something," he told Hailey. "After Cam's asleep."

Hailey wasn't sure what Winn wanted to discuss. But she had the feeling his struggles to get his project approved were going to seem like a walk in the park compared to the challenges of being a full-time father of a grieving boy.

Two hours later, Hailey relaxed against Winn's leather sofa, a glass of wine in one hand and the dog snoozing at her feet. The short walk had taken nearly an hour, with the three walking mostly in silence.

Winn had tried to draw the boy out but had quit attempting to make conversation when his efforts only seemed to agitate Cam.

They'd made it all the way to a downtown park that was lit up brighter than Times Square because of the ball game in progress. Cam hadn't wanted to watch the game or play on any of the equipment. But when Bandit picked up a stick and dropped it at Cam's feet, the boy had smiled and thrown it. Not once but several times.

Hailey had watched Cam smile each time the dog raced back to him, and her heart had filled with emotion.

"I don't know what I'm going to do, Hailey." Winn's expression was grave. "I have to work, but I can't just dump him somewhere with people I don't know or trust."

"What about your father?"

"Not an option."

His tone was so firm, Hailey let that possibility drop.

"You could take some time off," she suggested.

"This isn't a good time for me to do that." Winn dismissed the suggestion. "Besides, Cam will need to make friends."

"There are summer camps. Enrichment programs." Hailey chewed on her lip. "But the child just lost his mother. And this is a new place. I can't imagine tossing him into a group setting right away."

Winn twirled the stem of his wineglass between his fingers. "You mentioned the other day you were in the market for a job."

Hailey almost got whiplash from the change in topic. "You know someone who's looking for a speech therapist?"

"Me. You could also watch Cam for me. Just until he gets his footing and feels comfortable here."

"I help my dad with the ranch books," she told him. "I sometimes get called to the hospital if one of their regular speech therapists is ill. And I recently agreed to help Cassidy with weddings and special events. Workwise, I'm heating up."

"You could take him with you to your dad's. Cam would probably see it as a kind of adventure. I don't think he's ever spent time on a ranch." Winn's voice turned persuasive. "If you got called in to work at the hospital, I'd take that day off. Caring for him wouldn't be a long-term thing, only until Cam gets comfortable and I can make other arrangements."

"I appreciate your confidence, Winn. But—" She shook

her head. It sounded like babysitting to Hailey and she'd had her fill of that when she'd been in high school.

"I'd make it worth your while." Winn paused, considered. "I'd pay you—"

The amount he named had her jaw dropping. "Are you kidding me?"

"So you'll do it?"

She was tempted to say yes, but each time she acted in haste, it had never turned out well. "What hours would I work?"

"Negotiable," he said. "Monday through Friday during the day. Perhaps some nights and weekend hours if I had business functions to attend."

She could certainly use the money. Still, Hailey hesitated.

Winn surprised her by reaching out and taking her hand. The simple touch sent tingles up her arm.

"I have no intention of taking advantage, Hailey." His direct gaze fixed on hers. "Cameron is my son. I take my responsibilities seriously. I won't dump him on you. If it doesn't work, you can walk away any time. I'll be no worse off than I am now."

She had questions, lots of questions. Like why he'd been out of the boy's life for the past two years. But now wasn't the time, and it was difficult to think since his thumb had begun to stroke her palm. Almost impossible to form a logical thought—or question—when she was inhaling the intoxicating scent of his cologne.

This was her neighbor, she reminded herself. This was Winn, the man who'd dated many of her friends. Heck, he'd even taken out her sister-in-law before Anna and her brother had gotten involved.

"I'll toss in two free round-trip airline tickets to a destination of your choice," he told her, as if sensing her wavering.

It wasn't the money or airline tickets that tempted Hailey to say yes. It was the sound of muffled crying from down the hall, from a little boy in Avenger pj's who'd just lost his mother.

"I'll think about it," she promised Winn, "and give you my answer tomorrow."

Chapter Four

"Are you really going to work for Winn Ferris?" Anna Randall's voice rose.

Hailey looked around to see if anyone had overheard her sister-in-law. Although the streets of downtown Jackson were always filled with tourists, there were also local people who knew Anna was married to Hailey's brother, the mayor. Since Tripp had been elected last year, both Hailey and her sister-in-law were usually circumspect in their conversations. She must have really shocked Anna.

"I haven't decided." Hailey lifted a shoulder in a slight shrug. "Though I'm leaning toward saying yes."

Anna opened her mouth as if to say more when a ringing sounded from the depths of her eel-skin leather clutch. She raised one finger and eased out the phone. "I need to take this."

While Anna, a nurse-midwife, spoke with a labor-and-delivery nurse, they continued down the sidewalk. Despite her busy schedule, her sister-in-law always made time for Hailey. Every Tuesday they had a standing lunch date. The plans were sacrosanct and could only be broken for an emergency or a baby. From this side of the conversation, Hailey could tell Jackson Hole was about to welcome a new resident.

Anna strode down the concrete in her heels while Hailey hurried to keep pace in well-worn sneakers. The jeans and light sweater she'd pulled on that morning were in sharp contrast to Anna's studied elegance. Unlike Hailey, who was happiest being casual, her sister-in-law loved to dress up.

Despite her advancing pregnancy, Anna wore three-inch heels with a maternity dress in a color block of black, white and yellow. Her sister-in-law's chestnut hair tumbled to her shoulders and, as usual, her makeup was expertly applied. Hailey found her lips lifting in a rueful smile. If Cassidy wanted someone with elegance and styling acumen, she should hire Anna.

And Winn, wouldn't he do better having a mother type look after his son? Not that Hailey could imagine Winn knowing any "motherly" woman.

She'd spent a sleepless night tossing and turning, thinking of the little boy next door crying for his mother.

Anna dropped the phone back into her pocket. "Baby on the way. Luckily we're headed in the right direction."

Hailey glanced around, noting they'd left the quaint downtown area behind. Though not far from the center of town, the hospital was located in a predominantly residential area. Hailey calculated the distance and concluded they were only blocks from the small hospital that served Jackson Hole.

"I'll walk the rest of the way with you," she told Anna, when her sister-in-law wondered aloud why Hailey didn't turn toward her car. "I need to pick up my check."

The money for four days of work at the hospital last month wouldn't be much. Still, being able to provide speech therapy for both inpatients and outpatients kept her skills sharp and her foot in the door. Though she hoped a full-time position would open up, Hailey would have a good reference if she needed to eventually relocate.

"Tell me why you're considering watching the boy," Anna asked, bringing them back to their original conversation.

They continued to walk while Hailey explained Winn's dilemma in detail, as well as Cam's speech-therapy needs. "He needs someone to fill in until he can come up with a permanent solution. The money he offered was compelling."

When she mentioned the amount, Anna's eyes widened. Then she grinned. "Winn reminds me of his father. Both are convinced money can buy anyone or anything."

Though she knew Anna held no animosity toward the man she'd once dated casually, Hailey stiffened. "Winn understands I'd be putting my life on hold for the next few weeks to help him out. He wants to be fair."

Anna gave a little tinkle of a laugh. "I'd say that amount is more than fair."

"I'd like to help him." Though Hailey hadn't yet made her decision, she was leaning toward accepting the offer. "Besides, Cam is a sweet boy."

"If you do agree, don't let Winn suck you into being a 24/7 caregiver for the boy," Anna warned. "Ultimately the child is his responsibility, not yours."

"I know how to set boundaries," Hailey assured Anna. But when she thought of the small boy with the sad eyes and the man with the worried brow, she wasn't so sure.

Could the day get any worse?

Winn raked a hand through his hair. He should have convinced Hailey to start immediately rather than giving her time to think. He'd slept fitfully the night before. Memories of Vanessa and her quick smile clouded his thoughts and last night's dreams. Like Cam, he had difficulty accepting the fact that such a vibrant woman was gone.

Though Winn wasn't sure he'd loved Vanessa as much as he should have, she'd been Cameron's mother. Winn remembered how bereft he'd been when his own mother had died. He'd been twelve, older than Cam, but still a boy.

He was determined to give Cam the time and space he needed to grieve in his own way. Cam hadn't cried. Not at the funeral or on the way back to Jackson Hole. But last night Winn had stood outside the boy's bedroom and listened to the kid sobbing. He'd felt powerless and impotent. It wasn't a familiar feeling nor one he liked.

He'd considered going into the room to comfort the child but decided against the gesture. When Winn's mother died, the only tears he'd shed had been in the shower where no one could hear.

Today he and Cam would start a new life. Unfortunately, Winn wasn't sure how to begin. It had been two years since Vanessa had allowed him to see Cameron. The child he'd picked up in Atlanta was far different than the boy he'd once known.

Hot anger rose and threatened to boil over, but Winn firmly reminded himself the past couldn't be changed. And he bore some of the responsibility. He should have pushed harder.

Thankfully, sometime before dawn, Cam had fallen into an exhausted slumber. Despite his own lack of sleep, Winn had risen at six-thirty as usual. This gave him time to get dressed and make some calls before rousting Cam. One of those calls was to his father.

"Why do you have him?" His father sounded genuinely perplexed. "The child isn't—"

"In every way that matters, Cam is my son," Winn interrupted, his tone brooking no argument.

Jim Ferris must not have heard, because he bulldozed onward. "You haven't seen the kid in two years."

"Not for lack of trying." Winn clipped the words.

His father expelled an audible sigh. "I have connections at several top-notch boys' schools on the East Coast. He'd get a good education at any of them."

"I'm not sending a grieving little boy to strangers twenty-five hundred miles away," Winn protested, though he wasn't surprised by the suggestion. He remembered being shipped off shortly before he'd turned thirteen.

"You're a busy man," his father pointed out. "How are you going to tend to important business *and* watch a child?"

Winn briefly explained about Hailey and the temporary deal he'd offered.

"Smart move." His father's voice rang with approval.

"I believe so," Winn said. "Hailey is a warm person, which is what Cam needs right now. Plus—"

"I don't give a horse's backside if she's nice or not," Jim interrupted. "She's the mayor's sister. The closer you are to her, the closer you are to him. Take my advice. Don't try too hard to find a replacement. See if you can string this along until after the vote on the development."

Winn's grip tightened on his phone. The remark was classic Jim Ferris. His father was a wheeler-dealer who never missed an opportunity to manipulate a situation. But this advice had a stench. It reminded Winn of Josh and the way the weasel had used Hailey.

"I won't use Hailey to get closer to Tripp."

"You're a fool if you don't." His father's derision came through loud and clear. "And I didn't raise a fool."

"I—I heard a dog barking."

The plaintive voice had Winn turning. His heart tripped at the sight of a skinny boy in pajamas with his brown hair sticking up, standing barefoot in the hall.

"We'll talk later." Winn cut off the call and slipped the phone into the pocket of his black trousers. He rose to his feet, oddly unsteady. "Morning, champ. How'd you sleep?"

It was a stupid question. One the child didn't answer. Instead, Cam rubbed his eyes and glanced around the room. "Where's Bandit?"

Winn stepped cautiously toward the boy. "Next door."

He'd spotted Hailey leaving the complex on foot earlier… without the animal in tow.

"C-can we get him?"

There was something in the boy's eyes that Winn didn't like. A fearfulness, as if he expected to be slapped down for simply asking a question. During the six years he and Vanessa had informally shared custody of Cam, he'd never seen her strike out at the boy or raise her voice. But Brandon…

Winn's hands clenched into fists at his sides. If that man had hurt Cam…

He deliberately loosened his fists. If Brandon had mistreated Cam, there was nothing to be done about it now. The man was dead. His son was safe.

Winn placed a light hand on the boy's shoulder and relief flooded him when the child didn't pull away. "We'll eat first. By the time we finish, Hailey may be home and we can see if Bandit can…come over."

The thought of allowing that molting ball of slobber and fur back into his place made Winn cringe. But the dog and boy had formed a connection. When Bandit licked Cam's face last night, Winn had even seen a ghost of a smile on his son's lips.

"Okay." Cam stood there, as if unsure what to do next.

"Get some clothes on." Winn assumed boys of eight could be trusted to pick out proper attire. At six, Cam had been able to pull on his own clothes but had sometimes needed direction. "Jeans and a T-shirt should be adequate. We'll be spending most of the day here."

The boy nodded, took a few steps then turned back to Winn. "I—I shouldn't be with you."

Winn tilted his head. "Why not?"

"My dad said I d-d-don't belong with you."

Just hearing the boy call Brandon "his dad" had anger

rising inside Winn. He tamped it down. The past couldn't be undone. Because of Vanessa's duplicity, Cam had suffered. Winn would not add to the pain in those hazel eyes. "I'm your family now. I'm not going anywhere."

The boy only stared, a blank look on his face.

"I'm going to make chocolate-chip pancakes." Winn remembered they were a favorite of Cam's when he was younger. "You get dressed and I'll throw together some breakfast."

By the time Cam returned, dressed in a long-sleeved striped T-shirt and jeans, Winn had completed a couple of calls about a development in South Carolina that he was overseeing. He'd been distracted and made way too many pancakes.

When Cam had been a part of his life, Winn had done a little cooking, but since moving to Jackson Hole, business had been his priority. Everything else had taken a backseat.

Winn placed the plates on the table and sat down, prepared to get reacquainted with his son. As he unsuccessfully attempted to engage the boy in conversation, he realized his life had changed dramatically and he wasn't sure he was ready.

Hailey heard Bandit barking on her way up the steps to her second-floor condo and increased her pace. Although her rental agreement allowed pets, she knew the landlord wouldn't hesitate to act if her pet disturbed the other tenants.

She reached her door, hurriedly grabbing the key from her bag and fumbling with the lock. The barking escalated. "Bandit, shush."

"Hailey."

She heard Winn's voice but merely held up a hand and focused on opening the door. Dorianna Samuelson, on the other side of her, should be home from her yoga class any second. Even though the woman was a friend of Hailey's mother, she'd be the first to complain about the barking. Dorianna saw keeping the complex well ordered and quiet as her personal mission.

The dog gave a whimper of pleasure when he saw Hailey but followed her command to sit instead of jump, which had obviously been his impulse.

She grabbed the leash from the side table and clipped it on, before stepping back outside the door.

He looked business casual in black trousers, a gray shirt and shiny wing tips. Winn's lips curved in a slow smile that caused a fluttering in her belly.

Completely understandable, she told herself. A handsome man. A lazy smile. She'd have to be dead not to react.

The blood sliding through her veins like warm honey assured Hailey she was very much alive.

"Hey there, neighbor." She offered him a smile of her own. "Hope the barking didn't disturb you too much."

"It did." His eyes held an impish gleam. "But I know a way you can make it up to me."

The banter wasn't new, nor was the hint of electricity accompanying it. What surprised Hailey was her reaction, stronger than before. Keeping her hand firmly on the leash while the dog quivered at her side, she batted lashes at Winn. "What do you have in mind?"

Before Winn could respond, Cam stepped forward. His face lit up like a kid on Christmas morning when he saw the dog. A low whine formed in Bandit's throat.

Hailey loosened the retractable leash and said in a low tone, "Go to him."

The dog raced across the short distance and Cam's thin arms encircled him. The boy buried his face in the silky fur. Winn's eyes met Hailey's.

"That," he said, "was what you could do."

He gazed down at the boy with such affection in his eyes that Hailey felt tears sting the back of her lids. She quickly blinked them away.

Though she hadn't yet made up her mind about his offer, it was obvious Winn needed a friend to help him traverse this difficult time.

"I was thinking of heading out to my parents' ranch," she said in an offhand tone. "It's a nice day to ride horses, maybe have a picnic. You and Cam are welcome to join me."

Cam lifted his head at the mention of horses, but his hand remained firmly on the dog's back. "W-would Bandit come, too?"

Hailey nodded.

Winn glanced down at his tailored pants and shirt. "I'm not dressed for riding."

"Hmm." Hailey brought a finger to her lips. "You could change. Perhaps into something less stodgy."

Winn's dark brows winged up.

"Oops, I meant to say something more comfortable."

That brought a chuckle from Winn. "Give me a few minutes to make a couple of calls and get out of these 'stodgy' clothes."

Hailey's lips twitched before she turned her attention to the boy. "Cam, would you like to keep Bandit company while I toss together a picnic lunch?"

Cam's head jerked up and he glanced at his father.

"Up to you," Winn said.

"Okay."

The boy followed her into her condo and glanced around. She wondered if he noticed the difference between her overstuffed sofa with its colorful pillows and eclectic wall art and his father's perfectly decorated interior.

She doubted it. Cam was so focused on Bandit he barely gave anything around him a second glance. But when she pulled out French bread then started to cube some cheese, the boy moved to the counter to watch.

"I—I already ate," he stammered.

Though his eyes didn't meet hers, Hailey saw it as a

positive that the boy had initiated the conversation. "Riding horses always makes me hungry. I bet it makes you hungry, too."

Cam shrugged. After a couple of seconds, he took a tentative step forward.

"You smell good," he told her. "M-my mommy, sh-she smelled good, t-too."

Out of the corner of her eye, Hailey caught sight of Winn, who'd just entered her condo. He paused at Cam's words.

"You must miss her," Hailey murmured.

"Sh-she m-might be coming to get me." Cam looked up then and Hailey saw confusion and hope in his childish eyes. "P-people say she's dead. B-but what if she's looking for me? She m-might go to my house, but I—I won't be there. Sh-she w-w-won't know where I am."

It was a lot of words, filled with emotion and struggle. Hailey didn't interrupt and her heart ached at the underlying pain.

She swallowed hard against the lump in her throat and considered her response. Though undoubtedly this was something Winn should handle, the boy had shared his fears with *her*. It seemed wrong to ignore the question or redirect him to his dad.

"Your mother was a wonderful person who loved you very much." Hailey gentled her tone and met his gaze. "But she won't be coming back. Not because she wouldn't want to be with you, but she can't."

Tears spilled from those big sad hazel eyes and slipped down his cheeks. Answering ones welled in hers.

She placed a light hand on the small bony shoulder. "But your dad is here and—"

"M-my daddy is dead." Cam jerked away, clenching his small hands into fists at his sides.

"He isn't dead, honey," Hailey said gently, not bothering to hide her confusion. "Your dad is right behind you."

Cam turned. His jaw jutted up when his gaze settled on Winn. He shook his head. "That's not my dad."

Hailey saw Winn tense.

"Of course he is," Hailey protested.

"He's not," the boy doggedly insisted. "Mommy told me."

Chapter Five

Hailey's smile froze on her lips.

"Cameron. We'll discuss that later." Almost unrecogniz-able in worn jeans and a chambray shirt, Winn crossed the room and placed a hand on the boy's shoulder. "For now, I'd like you to take Bandit into the living room. I saw a brush on the coffee table. I bet Miss Hailey would like it if you'd brush him for her."

"That'd be wonderful." Confused, Hailey forced some enthusiasm into her voice. "Turn on the television if you'd like. Cartoons should be on one of the channels."

Cameron's gaze shifted from Hailey to his father and then to the dog. "C'mon, Bandit."

Sending the boy from the room didn't make sense to her. Why didn't Winn simply reassure Cam he was very much alive?

Once the sound of cartoon laughter and music filled the air, Hailey turned to Winn. She gestured with her head to-ward the living room. "What did he mean that his mother said you weren't his dad?"

"Do you have coffee?" Winn raked a hand through his hair, the gesture disturbing the expensive cut.

Hailey hesitated then moved to the counter and pulled out a tray of coffee pods. "What would you like?"

"Regular. Black."

She brewed a cup for him and then one for herself. After placing the mugs on the table, she took a seat opposite him and fixed her gaze on his face. "What's going on, Winn?"

"I didn't want to pull you into this right now, but since Cam brought it up and you may be watching him, you should know." Winn kept his voice low, though the sound from the other room made it impossible for Cam to hear even if he'd been speaking normally.

Winn took a sip of coffee and leaned back in the chair, but *relaxed* wasn't a word she'd use to describe him. Despite his bland expression, she could feel his restrained energy simmering in the air.

"I met Cam's mother at a party. She was a kindergarten teacher and a breath of fresh air compared to the type of women I normally dated." Winn relayed the information as if giving a business report to a board of directors. "We began dating, grew closer and became intimate. She mentioned Brandon only as a guy she'd once dated. As I'd had a couple semiserious relationships myself, I didn't think much of it."

Hailey sipped her coffee more for something to do than out of thirst.

Winn's gaze darkened. "We'd been together almost a year when things started heading south. I admit I'd let a project I was working on consume me, but she didn't even try to understand. Nothing I did pleased her. We argued constantly. After a big fight, she moved out. I called her a couple of times, but she didn't return my calls."

"When was this?" Hailey asked quietly.

"Almost nine years ago." He wrapped his hands around the ceramic mug. "Seven months later I learned from a friend Vanessa was pregnant and ready to deliver. I didn't doubt the baby was mine because we'd been together at the time he was conceived and Vanessa wasn't the kind to cheat."

The conversation was getting pretty doggone personal. She wondered if she should change the subject. Instead, she found herself asking, "What happened then?"

"I went to her. Confronted her. Demanded to know why she hadn't informed me she was pregnant." The hard opacity of his eyes was at odds with his matter-of-fact tone.

Though Hailey completely understood Winn's position, she shivered. She imagined he could be a formidable foe. "What did she say?"

Winn's jaw set in a rigid line. "Vanessa made it clear she didn't want to get back together, told me any feelings she had for me were gone."

"That didn't really answer your question," Hailey observed.

He shrugged. "I told her we'd made a baby and had to do what was best for him. I was in the delivery room when Cameron was born. We worked out an informal custody arrangement and child support. For six years we made a potentially difficult situation work with very little drama."

"Did you start dating each other again?" Hailey ventured.

"No." He expelled a heavy breath. "She was right. Whatever we had was over. Still, because of the baby, I was willing to try to see if we could get those feelings back. Vanessa wasn't interested. I even suggested we marry, but she nixed that, although my name was on the birth certificate and she put me in her will as guardian for Cam."

"Was that necessary? I mean, why did you need to be in the will? You were his dad." Something wasn't adding up.

"At the time I didn't think it was necessary, but since we weren't married, she insisted."

The water was still murky, but Hailey began to get a

slightly clearer picture. She wasn't surprised when Winn rose and began to pace.

While he strode across the room, Hailey attempted to put the pieces he'd given her together. "You said things worked well for six years. Then what happened?"

A muscle in his jaw jumped. He spat the name. "Brandon."

"The man who died in the accident with her?"

"He was also the same guy she'd dated before me." Winn's lip curled. "Turns out he wasn't as much of an ex as I thought."

Placing his hands on the counter, Winn leaned forward, his gaze focused out the window.

A sick feeling took up residence in the pit of Hailey's stomach.

"Apparently, around the time we were going through that rough patch, Vanessa had slept with him."

Though Winn did a stellar job of hiding it, there was pain underlying the words. Hailey's heart wrenched. But from the set look on his face, she knew Winn wouldn't appreciate her sympathy. She forced a nonchalant tone.

"Why did it take six years for him to show up?"

"He was engaged when he slept with Vanessa." His lips lifted in a sardonic smile. "His marriage lasted about seven years. He was still married when he ran into Vanessa having lunch with a friend in Buckhead. They began dating even before he'd separated from his wife."

Winn's voice was heavy with condemnation. Obviously he didn't condone extramarital affairs. For a second, Hailey wondered why she was so surprised. Then realized it was because Winn Ferris was a man who seemed to go after what he wanted, damn the consequences. This was a new side to him.

"S-so that bothered you?" To her horror, Hailey found herself stammering.

Winn didn't appear to notice.

"She dated a lot of men during those six years and so did I. Did I think it was wise for her to date a married guy? No. But it wasn't my business." Winn dropped into the chair. "I guess Brandon saw the birthmark on the back of Cam's neck and insisted they do a paternity test. I didn't know anything about it until they had the results."

The look on his face said it all.

"It showed Brandon was Cam's father," Hailey whispered.

"*Biological* father." Winn's voice snapped sharp as a whip. "*I* was his dad, the only one he'd ever known. That didn't seem to matter. Not to Brandon. And not enough to Vanessa for her to stand up for what was best for her son. Brandon wanted me out of Cam's life. Vanessa went along with his wishes."

"How could they cut you out?" Hailey's mind reeled. "Wasn't your name on the birth certificate?"

"Based on the paternity test, Vanessa petitioned to have it changed. One Sunday, I dropped Cam off after having him for the weekend and never saw him again." Winn rubbed the bridge of his nose as if trying to keep a headache at bay. "Calls went unreturned. Gifts were sent back unopened. It's no wonder Cam is confused and angry. One day I'm his daddy. The next, I'm gone, replaced by Brandon."

Hailey had so many questions she wasn't sure which one to ask first. "Vanessa wouldn't let you see Cam but left you in her will as his guardian? That doesn't make sense."

"Oversight, I'm sure." Winn gave a humorless laugh. "Brandon is probably rolling over in his grave right now. Don't get me wrong, I'm sorry Nessa is dead. But I wasn't a big fan of Brandon. The boy in the other room isn't the same child I raised for six years."

"The stammering is new."

Winn nodded. "He was six when I last saw him, talking a mile a minute, always had a smile on his face. He spoke easily, clearly."

"Did his fath—uh, did Brandon have a stutter?"

"Well, we weren't close," Winn said in a sarcastic tone. "But in our brief interactions, I never noticed one."

"Any idea when Cam's speech problems started?"

"Brandon's parents mentioned it was a fairly new occurrence."

"You're in contact with his parents?" Hailey couldn't keep the surprise from her voice.

"I picked Cam up from their house." Winn gave a tight smile. "They weren't pleased about having to hand him over to me."

"I imagine not," Hailey murmured, mentally sorting through the information she'd been given. Cam had no history of stuttering and the onset was recent. Both were good signs. As a speech therapist she knew Cam's part-word repetition, manifested by difficulty moving from the initial sound in the word, could be treated.

"It might be a good idea to have Cam evaluated by a physician. If the doctor believes the stuttering requires speech-therapy intervention, I'd be happy to help."

"I appreciate—" Winn began.

"When are we going to see the horses?"

Hailey glanced up and saw Cam in the doorway.

Winn offered the unsmiling child a wink. "We're ready to roll."

They'd reached the front door when Winn's phone rang. Hailey assumed he'd let it go to voice mail, but he held up a finger and took the call.

As the conversation lengthened, Cam tested out some ninja moves. Watching the boy, Hailey shifted from one foot to the other. She attempted to tune out what Winn was saying, but since she was standing right there, that proved impossible.

Apparently, negotiations on a new development in South

Carolina had hit a snag. It sounded as if whoever Winn was speaking with wanted him to fly down there and straighten things out. Winn mentioned Cam several times but seemed to be cut off before he got very far.

"I'll charter a flight out this afternoon," Winn replied to the person on the other end. "I'll be in touch once wheels are down."

Hailey stilled. Surely Winn wasn't thinking of leaving the state? Had he forgotten he had a child to consider?

"Sorry for the interruption." Winn pocketed the phone and flashed Hailey a rueful smile. "Looks like we have a change in plans."

Winn reached down and ruffled his son's hair. "We're not going to be able to ride horses today, sport. I need to take a quick trip out of town."

"You're leaving?" Though Cam had flashed accusing eyes at Winn only moments before, there was a plaintive quality to the boy's voice.

"Just a day or two." He offered the boy a reassuring smile. To his credit, Winn appeared truly regretful.

"Can I come with you?" Cam asked.

"Not this time."

Other than a trembling bottom lip, the boy stood absolutely motionless. "Who will watch me?"

Winn's gaze shifted to Hailey and he flashed a winning smile. "I'm hoping Miss Hailey will let you bunk with her and Bandit while I'm gone."

Hailey could almost see the wheels turning in the boy's head. As much as she liked Cam and wanted to help, the upcoming week was a busy one for her. Still, she *might* be able to make it work. She was flipping through her mental calendar, when Winn shrugged.

"If that doesn't work, my dad will keep you." Winn clapped a hand on Cam's shoulder.

Hailey was acquainted with Winn's self-centered father. The rancher made it his mission to steamroll anyone who stepped in his way. The only saving grace was his house-keeper, Elena. She was a wonderful woman who'd probably be the one to watch the boy. Hailey couldn't see Jim taking time from his "busy" schedule to babysit.

But Cam hadn't met Elena. The boy had barely set foot in Jackson Hole and if Hailey didn't agree to watch him, he'd be turned over to a stranger.

Cam's face blanched. "I—I don't know your dad."

"He's a nice man." Hailey forced a smile, hoping God wouldn't strike her dead for lying. "But you can meet him another time."

She turned to Winn. "Cam can hang with me and Bandit while you're out of town."

"Good." Relief crossed Winn's face. "Thanks."

He turned to his son. "I'll call as soon as I reach the hotel."

Cam stayed frozen in place while his dad went next door to pack.

Hailey's heart lurched when she saw Cam blinking back tears. She slung an arm around his shoulders. "Looks like it's you and me, buddy. What say we forget the picnic? Let's ride horses, then grab some pizza."

Though Winn had pushed through the business at hand, it was three days, not two, before he was able to return home. He'd called every night, eager to hear about his son's day. Cam always handed the phone over to Hailey after a minute or two.

Hailey's updates were filled with humorous anecdotes. It was obvious she'd been keeping Cam busy and having fun doing it.

Since Winn had made sure to let them know when to expect him back, he was surprised when Hailey came to his condo without Cam.

She was dressed casually in jeans and a blue-and-white-checkered shirt rolled up to her elbows, her bright smile a breath of fresh air. Setting his suitcase and briefcase on the floor, Winn dropped wearily into the closest chair. "Where's Cam?"

"At Travis and Mary Karen Fisher's," Hailey said, referring to a couple with five children, four of them rambunctious boys. "It's Logan's birthday. They invited Cam to his party. I figured you wouldn't mind."

"No. I don't." Winn pulled his brows together. Travis's herd of curly-haired boys blended together in his mind. "Logan?"

"Their middle son." Hailey gestured toward the kitchen. "Can I get you some coffee? Then I'd like for us to talk."

Though her tone was light, something told him he might not like what she had to say. "Thanks, but I need something stronger."

Rising to his feet, Winn pulled out a bottle of whiskey from a liquor cabinet and poured himself a drink. She shook her head when he lifted the bottle.

"How's Cam today?" He brought the glass to his lips. She wanted to talk so they'd talk. But he had a few questions of his own first. "He barely said two words to me on the phone."

"I tried to prompt him to talk but he clammed up. I think—" she paused and spoke slowly as if choosing her words carefully "—having you leave so soon after he got here was difficult for him."

Though her tone held no censure, Winn stiffened. He hated that he'd caused the boy pain. Then he thought of the delicate business negotiations he'd handled in South Carolina. A lot of money had been at stake. Not to mention his standing at GPG Investment. He took a long drink. "Couldn't be helped," he muttered.

Hailey's eyes darkened, reminding him of the turbulent seas off the Charleston coast last night. When she spoke, her voice was soft, so faint Winn had to strain to hear. "We always have a choice."

It was an arguable point, but Winn wasn't in the mood for a debate. Damn, he was exhausted. "This was a crisis."

"Your son needed you." Tiny lines bracketed her eyes and he realized suddenly she looked as tired as he felt. He wondered if Cam had kept her up at night, crying for his mother.

Winn felt a ripple of unease. "I knew I could trust him with you."

"What about your father?" Hailey's brow arched. "Would you have trusted Cam with him?"

Winn hesitated. He was under no illusions concerning his father. But he trusted Elena and the last-minute business trip had left him few options.

"If I hadn't agreed to watch Cam, you'd have sent him to a strange place only days after his mother's funeral."

Winn's temper spiked. "If you had other obligations or didn't want to do keep him, you should have said no."

Hailey expelled a heavy sigh and ran a hand through her wavy blond hair. If not for the fatigue in her eyes, she could be a college girl ready for a day of fun.

"Cam is struggling, Winn." She met his gaze, her eyes steady and very blue. "He needs his dad. Not me. Certainly not some stranger."

"Thanks for giving me the benefit of your vast parenting experience." He knew his tone was slightly mocking but she'd hit a nerve.

Instead of snapping back, her gaze searched his, the lines of worry deepening. "You love Cam. I don't doubt that for a second. I see it in the way you look at him and the kindness you show him. You have it in you to be a fabulous dad. But the boy is hurting and he doesn't trust you. As hard as this may seem, you have to let him come to you first."

For a Saturday morning, the bike trail was surprisingly deserted. Winn had borrowed a couple of Treks hoping to find a way to connect with his son. He'd told his superiors at GPG Investment he was taking a few days off.

Though it had been only two years since he'd shared custody of Cam, he'd forgotten the time it took to care for a child. Not to mention how frustrating it was to live with a boy who seemed determined to keep him at arm's length.

As they pedaled down the concrete trail at the base of the mountains, Winn's mind kept returning to Hailey's comment about him needing to act like a dad and make Cam a priority.

He thought of the sitter he'd lined up for tonight. He hadn't wanted to leave Cam so soon after he'd returned from South Carolina, but he'd accepted Clive's invitation to his daughter's wedding months before. It didn't matter that it was only a social occasion. Truth was, more business was done on golf courses and at parties than in boardrooms and offices.

Tonight would be a chance for Elena and Cam to become acquainted. Winn hadn't been able to bring himself to ask Hailey to watch his son.

Winn stifled a curse. Things had never been this difficult in Atlanta. Recalling those days, he realized part of the reason they'd gone without a hitch was because Vanessa had always been there. Even on the days he was supposed to have Cam, if he had a sudden business trip or an unexpected meeting, Vanessa had been happy to step in.

Unlike Hailey, Vanessa had never brought up the issue of his priorities. Of course, she'd also been Cam's mother.

Winn cast a sideways glance at the skinny child riding beside him on the path. With his jeans, graphic T-shirt and ball cap, Cam looked like any eight-year-old enjoying a sunny summer day with his dad. But Cam had been through a lot in his young life. More than most adults. No wonder he stuttered.

The realization saddened Winn. He'd recently made an appointment with Kate Dennes, a local pediatrician and friend. He hoped she'd give him some tips on how to reach his child, since she had a daughter about the same age.

"What do you think of the mountains?" he asked Cam, suddenly impatient with the silence between them.

"B-big." The boy slanted a sideways glance. "C-can I see Bandit today?"

It wasn't the first time Cam had asked about the dog. But Hailey and the animal hadn't been around much the past two days.

Winn wondered if she'd just been busy or if Hailey was avoiding him. Because of her concern over his Charleston trip, he hadn't asked what she'd decided about watching Cam full-time.

He needed to get her answer soon. If she said no, he might have to "borrow" Elena until he found the right person. Considering how proprietary his father was about his housekeeper, having her watch Cam for even a short time could be problematic.

"C-can Bandit c-come over and play?" Cam pressed when Winn didn't answer.

"When we get home, I'll call Hailey and see."

The quicksilver smile the boy flashed warmed his heart as they turned the bikes in the direction of the car. Winn felt his own spirits lift.

He'd missed seeing Hailey the past two days. Unfortunately, he knew his neighbor wouldn't be pleased when she learned he was leaving Cam with a sitter for the evening. He could almost hear her asking why he didn't take the child with him.

Winn cast a sideways glance at the boy. Though he wasn't one to mix business with pleasure, he knew there would be children in attendance. This morning when he'd run into Cole at Hill of Beans, the entrepreneur had mentioned he and his wife would be at the festivities tonight, along with their two children.

"Hey, Cam," Winn said when they neared the parking

lot where the truck he'd borrowed from his father sat. It was shiny and black and so big it might as well have been a tank. But that was his dad; the man never did anything in half measures. "Interested in attending a party with your old man tonight?"

Chapter Six

The ceremony had been beautiful, with miles of white tulle, hundreds of fragrant flowers and a bright summer sky. Cassidy and Daffy had worked their magic on the bride and her eight attendants' hair; Hailey had been in charge of makeup.

It had been an enjoyable day, laughing and talking with women who were close to her own age, while enhancing their natural beauty. Yet, even as Hailey had consulted on colors that best suited each girl and applied mascara, eye shadow and foundation, her thoughts kept returning to Winn and Cam.

Her neighbors remained on her mind even as Hailey strolled to the reception tent with Cassidy after all the pictures had been taken. Touching up hair and makeup during the postceremony wedding pics had been part of the salon package. She wondered how Winn was handling being a father again, and if Cam had begun to feel more comfortable around the man who he believed abandoned him.

A niggle of guilt tugged at her. Had she been too unfeeling with Winn? Had she not tried hard enough to see the situation from his perspective?

"It was nice of the Finsters to invite us to the reception." Cassidy grabbed two glasses of champagne from a passing waiter. She handed one to Hailey, keeping one for herself.

Hailey took a sip from the flute. "Why did Daffy rush off?"

"Our Daffodil loves people but not crowds." Cassidy's gaze slid around the large tent with the shiny wooden dance floor. Men in dark suits and women in cocktail dresses laughed and danced and drank champagne.

"I love parties." Hailey stood with Cassidy at the edge of the tent, surveying the crowd as they talked over the music and din of other conversations.

"These are your peeps," Cassidy mused aloud. "You and Susan, our beautiful bride, graduated together."

Hailey considered reminding Cassidy she'd graduated from Jackson Hole High, too. "Sue raved about her hair."

"She seemed jazzed with her makeup, as well," Cassidy said smugly. "You and I, chickadee, are a Zumba of a team. We're going to make boatloads of moola."

Zumba of a team?

Surely Cass realized Zumba was an aerobic-fitness program not an adjective. But knowing Cassidy, she was well aware of that fact. Knew and didn't care. The woman always marched to her own drummer. Hailey grinned. "It's cool to get paid while doing something I enjoy."

"Grapevine says Winn Ferris has a kid."

Hailey was surprised she didn't have whiplash. This, she realized, was what the hairstylist really wanted to discuss. She wondered why it had taken so long for her friend to bring up the subject. Of course, this was the first opportunity they'd had to talk privately since they'd arrived at the ranch.

They'd been too busy doing hair and makeup and chatting with the wedding party to have any kind of personal conversation. Despite her outlandish style—today Cassidy wore pink pants so tight they looked painted on, coupled with a canary-yellow top complete with feathers—she was a businesswoman first.

"Hel-lo," Cassidy said when Hailey took another sip of champagne. "I spoke, now it's your turn. That's how this conversation thingy works."

"Yes, Winn has a little boy," Hailey confirmed. "He's eight. His name is Cameron. He's a real cutie."

"The mother?"

"She died recently in a boating accident."

"Don't you find it interesting he never mentioned having a kid?" Cassidy's finely tweezed eyebrow arched behind her yellow-and-black cat's-eye glasses.

Though Hailey liked to gossip as much anyone, she found herself seized with an urge to change the subject. "I suppose so. But—"

"Why do you think he clammed?"

Cassidy was like a dog with a bone. Not just any dog. Bandit would easily give up his bone if she asked nicely. Cass was like a pit bull. Her jaws were clamped tightly around this bone, er, topic. Hailey would have to come up with something very interesting to distract Cassidy.

Hailey glanced around and tossed a Hail Mary. "Oh, look, there's Liam Gallagher. We dated back in high school. I heard he was back in town."

Cassidy turned her head and followed Hailey's gaze. She wasn't certain if Cass would remember Liam from Jackson Hole High, but the hairstylist's gaze pinned him almost immediately.

Tall and lean, with his wavy hair slightly tousled, Liam wore a navy suit with a crisp white shirt and red tie. Hugging his muscular shoulders and tapering down to his lean waist, the fit was incredible. The past decade had been good to him.

As a boy he'd been all arms and legs, with an angular face that had been more interesting than handsome. In the years Liam had been gone from Jackson Hole, he'd turned from boy to man. There were muscles beneath that suit, and the features of the angular face were now chiseled and all male.

Cassidy gave a low whistle. "Like a fine wine…"

The hairstylist's voice trailed off as she continued to stare.

"He's a real hottie, right?" Hailey said, sensing the bone loosening from Cassidy's slack jaws.

"Is he…single?"

"Did you just lick your lips?"

Cassidy waved her hand in an impatient gesture. "Answer the question."

"I believe so," Hailey said slowly. "Mrs. Samuelson keeps in contact with his mother, Janice. Apparently, his mom was upset he'd recently broken it off with Ms. Perfect."

"Dorianna always has the inside scoop," Cassidy said. "I look forward to her visits to the salon for that reason alone."

"Did I tell you she complained to my landlord about Bandit's barking?"

"Hold that thought." Cassidy grabbed her arm and Hailey found herself being hauled through the crowd in the direction of her former crush. "It's time you and I got reacquainted with Luscious Liam."

Conscious of the child at his side, Winn cut his conversation with Merle Bach short. The portly white-haired gentleman, who bore a distinct resemblance to Santa Claus, might appear jovial, but beneath that genial smile was a serpent who could strike at any time. Still, as a friend of Winn's father and a member of the board of trustees, Merle could be counted on to do whatever he could to push Winn's golf-course development through the approval process.

Winn slanted a glance at Cam, who was silently surveying the throng of people. Remembering how he'd hated the suits his father had made him wear from a young age, Winn had picked out a pair of khakis and a madras plaid shirt for his son to wear this evening.

Two long years separated them now. The closeness they'd once shared seemed out of reach. He cursed Brandon under his breath.

Cam's biological father hadn't wanted Winn to play any part in Cam's life. Insecure, yet at the same time supremely arrogant, Brandon decreed a boy only needed one father and that would be him.

When Brandon told Winn he should be relieved to be off the hook, Winn knew the man would never understand.

Anger sluiced through his veins. If Brandon had allowed him to remain involved in Cam's life, he wouldn't be a stranger now. And Cam wouldn't be alone with his grief.

Summoning a hearty voice, Winn tousled the boy's hair. "Would you like another piece of cake, sport?"

The boy shook his head but didn't pull away. Though he refused to hold Winn's hand, Cam had been glued to his side since they'd arrived.

"Ferris," someone called out.

Winn turned to see Cole Lassiter, dressed in a dark tailored suit. At his side was his wife, Meg, a tall slender woman with auburn hair. She had a toddler in her arms. Beside them was a boy who was the spitting image of his father. Winn's unpracticed eye judged him to be close to Cam's age.

"I wasn't sure we'd see you here," Cole said by way of greeting, his curious gaze darting to Cameron. "Who is this with you?"

Winn placed his hand lightly on Cam's shoulder. "This is my son, Cameron."

He could feel Cam's shoulders stiffen, but the boy remained silent.

"It's nice to meet you, Cameron." Meg glanced at her son, who was dressed similarly to Cam but in dark pants and a polo shirt. "I bet you and Charlie are about the same age."

"I-I'm eight," Cam said.

Cole glanced at his son. "So is Charlie."

"We were just headed to the children's tent," Meg said. "Perhaps Cam would like to come with us?"

At Winn's curious glance, Meg smiled. "The Finster family hired several high-school girls to supervise the grade-school children so the parents could more easily mingle. They have all kinds of games."

"We looked. They have video games," Charlie interrupted. The boy's gray eyes held a mischievous glint as they settled on Cam. "Wanna play? Bet I can beat you."

"Charlie," Meg said in a stern voice, but her husband just laughed.

Winn caught his son's inquiring look. "If you want to go, you can."

The boy nodded.

"I'll make sure they're settled," she told Winn and Cole as the toddler in her arms began to squirm. "I wish they had a tent for the younger ones, too."

"Evie and I want to fly." Cole scooped the girl in the white frilly dress out of his wife's arms and sent the child flying through the air. Evie broke out in giggles, not seeming to notice her mother leaving with the two boys.

Winn only hoped whoever was watching the children could be trusted.

"Don't worry." Cole clapped a hand on Winn's back. "Meg is very particular. She'll make sure the boys are safe."

Winn shifted his gaze back to Cole. "Cam isn't very social. His mother died recently and he's having difficulty adjusting."

"I understand." The look in Cole's eyes told Winn he

did. "You weren't in Jackson Hole when Charlie came to live with me and Meg. We weren't married then."

Winn inclined his head. "I thought Charlie was your son?"

"He's mine." Cole spoke firmly in a matter-of-fact tone. "But he lived the first part of his life with his mother, Joy, and her husband, Ty. They were both my close friends and were killed in a car accident on Route 22. Meg and I were given joint custody."

Winn hesitated, thinking about the past week. "That had to be difficult."

Cole gave a robust laugh. "You're a master of understatement, Ferris."

"I'm only starting down the road you've already traveled," Winn admitted. "I wish there was an app I could download on parenting a grieving boy."

"If you find one, be sure to let me know." The expression in Cole's eyes turned from laughter to serious. "The best advice I can give on parenting is to get your priorities straight and do your best."

"That's helpful," Winn said drily.

"Think about it, if you do your best, putting the welfare of your son first, you'll have no regrets." Cole lifted his girl into the air and she squealed.

Though Winn had been in Jackson Hole over a year, this was the first conversation he'd had with Cole where he'd felt connected. Whenever they'd spoken before, it had always been superficial.

Winn was prepared to bring up his child-care dilemma when Meg returned.

"I'll take her." Meg hefted the squirmy, redheaded toddler from her husband's arms. "If I put her down, she'll take off for Colorado. Evie recently mastered walking. Of course, our little angel isn't content to walk, she wants to run. Like her dad, she has only one speed—full out."

Cole poked his wife teasingly. "Any ambulation issues are from you, my dear physical therapist."

Meg rolled her eyes then turned her attention to Winn. "Cameron and Charlie are getting along great. I'd like to have him over sometime to play."

"Name the date and time." Winn found himself strangely touched by the offer.

"I'll check my calendar and give you a call," Meg said, then appeared to notice the direction of her husband's gaze.

"That man that Hailey is talking to," Cole said half to himself. "He looks familiar."

At the mention of Hailey's name, Winn turned and followed Cole's gaze. Hailey looked stunning in vivid blue. Cassidy, as brightly colored as any Amazon parrot in paisley swirls, stood talking to a man Winn didn't recognize.

Winn guessed him as late twenties and successful at whatever he did. His suit was perfectly tailored. He and the two women were engaged in an animated conversation with lots of hand gestures and laughter.

Winn couldn't help noticing the guy's attention kept returning to Hailey. That, Winn understood. The silky blue dress she wore flattered her compact but curvy figure. "Who is he?"

Meg narrowed her gaze and a thoughtful look crossed her face. "I believe he graduated with one of my younger brothers."

Cole tickled his daughter playfully, making her chortle. "Considering all your younger brothers, that hardly narrows it down."

"Liam." Meg snapped her fingers, triumph lighting her eyes. "Liam Gallagher. I heard he was back in Jackson."

"Where has he been?" Winn's eyes narrowed as the man sidled even closer to Hailey.

"Someone told me he's here to help Pete Allman in his psychology practice until Pete can find a permanent associate," Cole mused aloud.

"I heard he came back to help his great-aunt," Meg interjected.

"Perhaps he's doing both," Winn stated. From the way the guy was looking at Hailey, seducing the pretty speech therapist appeared to be another item on the man's to-do list.

Hailey spent most of the evening on the dance floor. She'd forgotten how much fun it was to simply move to the music, especially after a couple of glasses of French champagne.

She danced with many men, but mostly with Liam. The band had started a slow, romantic set when Winn tapped Liam on the shoulder. He smiled at Hailey. "May I have this dance?"

To Hailey's surprise, Liam hesitated, holding on to her hand for an extra beat. But Winn didn't appear to notice. He took her into his arms with well-practiced ease then maneuvered her across the dance floor until Liam was out of sight.

"You're looking lovely this evening," Winn remarked.

"You look quite dashing yourself." Hailey thought he smelled even better. She inhaled and let the spicy masculine scent of his cologne travel leisurely through her system. "I didn't expect to see you here tonight."

"I guess we're both surprised."

"Who's watching Cam?"

"Some high-school girl."

"What's her name?" Hailey asked, curious. "I might know her family."

"I don't know her name."

Hailey came to a dead stop in his arms. "You left him with a girl whose name you don't even know?"

Though she tried to control it, her voice rose with every word.

"Easy, tiger," he said with an amused smile. "I brought

Cam with me. He's at the children's tent with Charlie Lassiter. They're playing video games. Meg vouched for the security."

"Oh." Warmth rose up Hailey's cheeks. *So much for jumping to conclusions.* As a speech therapist, it was natural for her to want to be protective of a child. But her concern felt more personal. She told herself to stop overreacting. It wasn't fair to Winn.

Hailey relaxed as they moved across the floor in perfect synchronicity.

"I believe you owe me an apology. I didn't leave my son with a stranger."

She looked up into the eyes that were riveted on her face. Until this moment she hadn't realized there were flecks of gold in his hazel depths.

"Such beautiful eyes," she murmured.

"Pardon me?"

Hailey jolted as she realized with sudden horror that she'd spoken aloud. Thankfully, he didn't appear to have made out the words. "Ah, sorry."

His lips twitched, but he merely continued to move her across the dance floor, his body hard against hers. "You didn't mention how you happened to be here. Are you friends of the bride or groom?"

"I'm a business associate of the bride's dad." Winn easily moved Hailey into an intricate turn.

Her breath caught in her throat as the move pressed her even more tightly against him. "Makeup artist for the wedding party."

Winn shot her a dazed look "That's quite a job."

"Not only a job but a heckuva lot of work." Hailey smiled ruefully. "There are eight bridesmaids."

Winn wasn't sure how many most women had, but he assumed eight was excessive. Still, he didn't ask. Makeup had never been a favorite conversation topic. "I spoke with Cassidy."

Actually, she'd strolled up and told him he owed her a dance. He hadn't argued. Though Winn had never been into avant-garde, he admired Cassidy's drive and enjoyed her eclectic fashion style.

"I noticed the two of you out on the dance floor earlier." Hailey's lips quirked. "You do a mean mambo, my friend."

"Cassidy deserves all the credit." The twinkle in his eyes made Hailey's blood course through her veins like warm honey. "I simply followed her lead."

"Don't give me that." Hailey's voice took on a teasing lilt. "Winn Ferris forges his own way. He leads. He doesn't follow."

Mock horror crossed his face. "You sound like my father."

"Don't be mean, Winn," she warned, her voice a sexy rumble.

He brushed a tendril of hair back from her face then leaned forward, his breath warm against her ear. "I could never be mean to you."

Her eyes darkened and she lifted her head. So close that her mouth hovered mere inches from his.

"Glad you could make it, Ferris."

Winn jerked back and turned, burying his irritation beneath an easy smile. "Clive."

Clive Finster, the bride's father, reminded Winn of a jaunty penguin in black tie. Short and stubby, he had more hair in his well-groomed goatee than on his entire head. His wife, a brittle-looking blonde who towered over her husband by a good five inches, heaved a resigned sigh.

Winn had the feeling Clive had been stopping nearly every guest to chat.

"I appreciated the invitation." Winn smiled at Mrs. Finster. "Your daughter was a beautiful bride. And I'm enjoying the reception."

Dee Finster smiled politely. "We were relieved the weather cooperated."

"It was a perfect day," Hailey said.

For the first time, Clive appeared to notice her. Winn saw when he made the connection. "Hailey Randall. Frank's daughter."

Tripp's sister, Winn could almost hear him add.

Clive belonged to the Jim-Ferris-School-of-Business, the one that touted if you didn't take the lead you deserved to be ground into the dust. The man's gaze sharpened as it shifted between her and Winn. "I didn't realize the two of you were—"

"Winn and I are neighbors." Hailey spoke quickly before Winn had a chance to respond. "And I'm watching his son this summer until he finds a permanent sitter."

Winn's heart jumped like a thousand-pound marlin. He covered his surprise with a bland expression that gave nothing away.

Clive's smile broadened, but when he opened his mouth to speak, his wife placed a hand on his arm. "Merle and Helen are coming this way. Didn't you say you wanted to speak with him this evening?"

"Indeed I do. Great to see you again, Ferris. Ms. Randall." The amenities concluded, Clive turned his attention on a bigger fish in the pond.

"I never could understand how someone as nice as Susan could come from a father like that," Hailey said in a low tone as they resumed dancing.

Winn grinned. "I take it you're not a Clive fan."

Hailey gave a snort. "The man is a bottom-feeder."

"Why don't you tell me how you really feel?" Winn began then stopped himself. "Better yet, tell me what made you decide to watch Cam?"

Chapter Seven

"The reason I decided to watch Cam…" Hailey's head jerked up as the band launched into a Gershwin classic. Impulsively she grabbed Winn's hand. "Dance with me first. I love this one."

Though he willingly followed her to the dance floor, once he'd taken her into his arms, he quirked a brow. "The melody reminds me of something from my father's, or even my grandfather's, era."

As they moved in time to the slow, romantic rhythm, Hailey explained that her parents loved to dance to "Embraceable You" and let him in on a little secret.

"This was played at my grandparents' wedding. My parents kind of adopted the song." Hailey couldn't keep from smiling. "Growing up, I'd stroll into a room and find my mom with her head on my dad's shoulder. They'd be dancing to this song playing from my dad's boom box."

"Shocking," Winn said with an exaggerated shudder. "What were they thinking?"

"Probably that they wished I was off playing with a friend." Hailey smiled wryly and made him chuckle.

As a child she'd been mortified. Now she thought it sweet that, after playing together as toddlers and marrying straight out of college, her parents were still so much in love.

Privately, Hailey hoped to one day enjoy that same closeness with her husband. Tripp had found it during his short-lived marriage to Gayle, his childhood sweetheart. Sadly, Gayle and their unborn baby had died due to pregnancy complications.

Several years later her brother had seen Anna—whom he'd known his entire life—in a different light, and they were now blissfully happy. Was falling in love with someone you'd known since childhood the secret?

Trouble was, there weren't many men she'd known from way back who weren't already engaged or married. Other than Tim Duggan, now a widower with two little girls, or—

"You were lucky. My parents could barely stand to be in the same room." Winn spoke in a matter-of-fact tone. "There was no love between them for as far back as I can remember. My father even scheduled a business meeting the afternoon of her funeral."

Hailey unsuccessfully attempted to hide her shock. "How old were you?"

"Twelve."

At that age Hailey's biggest worry had been not falling off her horse during barrel-racing practice. "I'm sorry, Winn."

He shrugged as if it was of no consequence and fell silent.

The music weaved around them like a pretty ribbon. Hailey rested her head on Winn's chest, holding him tightly, as if she could protect him from past pain.

She closed her eyes and let her mind drift, loving the feel of his strong arms around her. When his movements slowed, she reluctantly opened her eyes and realized the song had ended. Not only that, the band had left the raised platform for a break.

Hailey lifted a perfectly manicured hand in an airy wave to hide her embarrassment and stepped from Winn's arms. "I like to dance until the very last note."

"Lucky me."

She cocked her head.

"I got to hold a beautiful woman a little longer." He took her hand. The desire she'd been fighting all evening ignited.

From the moment she first met Winn, his all-business, buttoned-up look had turned her on. Even the way he smelled—like spice and soap—was a potent aphrodisiac. Not to mention his body, so firm and hard against hers, had stirred all sorts of feelings. Feelings that refused to fade, even though they weren't pressed tightly together anymore.

As they strolled through the crowd, Hailey wondered what it'd be like to unbutton that pristine white shirt, tug it from the waistband of those perfectly tailored trousers and wrap her hand around his hot, bare flesh.

Her body shivered with longing. She hadn't been with a man since she'd arrived in Jackson Hole, but she had a feeling Winn would surpass anyone she'd—

"Hailey, how nice to see you this evening."

She inhaled sharply, the dampness between her thighs turning as dry as the Mohave.

"Pastor." Hailey buried naked images of Winn behind a sweet smile. "I assume you know Winston Ferris."

Discovering Winn and the minister were *not* acquainted necessitated introductions, which Hailey quickly performed.

She dragged out the conversation a little longer than was absolutely necessary, not only commending the slender gray-haired man on his part in the marriage ceremony earlier, but also bringing up recent sermons.

Winn participated superficially, but kept slanting glances

at her as if trying to figure out why she was lingering. He couldn't know she was fighting the urge to suggest they find someplace private.

Blame it on the wedding, she thought ruefully. A handsome man, the intoxicating scent of fresh flowers and seeing a couple so much in love saying their vows had filled the air with romance. It had also brought back the memory of the single kiss she'd once shared with Winn.

It had been a long time ago, over a silly party game of Spin the Bottle. But he'd made it a kiss to remember.

Of course, her memory might have embellished the impact, but Hailey didn't think so. The way she was feeling tonight, one kiss of that caliber could easily tumble her straight into Winn's bed.

Even as she experienced a thrill at the thought, Hailey knew it wasn't going to happen. She'd never been into one-night stands. And Winn wasn't into relationships.

After a couple minutes, the groom drew the pastor away. Winn wasted no time directing Hailey with purposeful steps across the reception tent and into the quiet of the warm summer evening.

Outside, they followed a crushed-rock path and settled on an ornate metal bench under a large oak. Winn looped his arm casually along the back of the bench.

He surprised her by raising his eyes to the skies and expelling a heavy breath. "Thank you, God."

"Okay, I'll bite." Hailey laughed. "What are you thanking him for?"

"I was convinced the preacher was going to ask me which of the sermons you were discussing was *my* favorite." Winn shook his head. "That would have been disastrous. I'm not good at that kind of thing."

"From what I've observed, Mr. Ferris, you're very adept at thinking on your feet."

"I'm excellent," he said with no pretense of modesty.

"I was speaking of my ability to come up with answers to sermon questions."

"Too much of a sinner?" she teased.

His lips lifted in a lazy smile and he fingered a lock of her hair, rubbing a silky strand between a thumb and forefinger. "Is gluttony a sin?"

Something in his eyes told her he wasn't speaking about food. She swallowed past the sudden dryness in her throat and nodded.

"Well, I've been known to overindulge on occasion."

Hailey let her gaze linger on his mouth, on those sensual lips. She could only imagine all the ways he *indulged*. Though the evening was mild, gooseflesh dotted her exposed skin. Electricity filled the air.

An answering spark flared in Winn's dark eyes.

Hailey found herself leaning toward him with tingling lips, but she pulled back before reaching the point of no return. All too easily she could find herself indulging in *him*. Drastic measures were needed to prevent that from happening.

"To answer your earlier question, I'm not sure exactly when I decided to watch Cam." Hailey had observed discussing a child or a baby was a great way to kill any lascivious thoughts.

It appeared to work on Winn. The smoldering heat in his eyes vanished as if she'd doused him with a bucket of cold water.

She experienced a pang of regret before continuing. After all, she liked *indulging* as much as any other young, single woman. "I was leaning toward saying yes when you first asked me to watch him. Since then I've been impressed with your desire to help Cam adjust and I want to help."

"Thank you."

His hand closing over hers had her rising to her feet. She spoke casually over the loud thumping of her heart.

"If you're checking on Cam, I'd love to come with you. If you don't mind, that is."

"Of course I don't mind. I enjoy your company."

Deciding she had her emotions under control, Hailey took his proffered arm. Still, she couldn't stop the pleasure that washed over her when he smiled down at her.

"I've been to my share of weddings," Winn said as they drew close to the small tent located near the Finster home. "I don't recall ever seeing a children's tent."

"This is a first for me, too," Hailey admitted. "I heard the Finsters have a huge contingent of family here, most of whom brought their children. Mrs. Finster didn't want them running wild and decided to provide a supervised area. Susan convinced her mother to open the tent to the kids of wedding attendees."

The tent holding the children was much smaller than the one for the adults. Instead of an archway decorated with flowers and tulle, the entrance to this tent had a huge banner proclaiming May the Force Be With You. Laughter and shouts from the interior spilled into the calm night air.

A teenage girl dressed as Princess Leia was texting while standing guard. Her dark hair was wound into a bun on one side. Only because she was looking did Hailey see the look of startled surprise in Winn's eyes as they drew close.

But as he approached the "princess," his expression gave nothing away. "I'm here to check on my son."

The girl stuffed the phone in her pocket and stepped aside. She smiled, showing a mouthful of braces. "If he's inside, I'm sure he's having fun."

Upon entering the tent, Hailey's eyes were drawn to the tables of food. She saw "Jedi Juice" and bottles of "Vaderade." The Jabba the Hutt cake looked as if it had been set upon by a swarm of locusts. The Obi-Wan Kenobies made out of fruit had barely been touched. Hailey grabbed a "Wookiee Cookie" and popped it into her mouth, while glow stars and planets glittered overhead.

The original *Star Wars* movie played in one corner. Children watched from multicolored beanbag chairs in front of the big screen. A group of younger children played Pin the Lightsaber on Yoda, with the help of a girl dressed as Luke Skywalker.

Another group of school-age boys and girls sat around a table building a Lego starfighter.

She spotted Cam at the same time as Winn. Blindfolded under a Darth Vader piñata, his son swung a lightsaber with all his might at the papier-mâché container while a group of boys cheered him on. With a solid *thwack,* the piñata opened and candy spilled out. Cam whipped off his blindfold and grinned triumphantly at Charlie, before both boys dived for the treats.

Hailey had never seen Cam smile so broadly, not even for Bandit. She slanted a sideways glance at Winn. Her heart rose to her throat at the look on his face.

This, she realized, was why she'd agreed to help him. He wanted nothing more than for his son to be happy, and it was within her power to help him succeed. This was her opportunity to make a difference.

While a few kids scrambled for the last of the goodies, a girl dressed in a Chewbacca fur bodysuit and mask, blindfolded Logan, Travis and Mary Karen's middle boy. His twin brothers shouted encouragement from the sidelines.

Hailey waited by the food table, trying one of the fruit kabobs and watched Logan's wild swings. Hailey couldn't believe the money the Finsters had spent to keep the children happy.

Perhaps, Hailey mused, she'd missed her calling. Maybe she should consider adding party planning to her list of part-time jobs. When she'd left her promising career as a speech therapist in Denver to return to Jackson, she never thought she'd have such difficulty finding a full-time professional position.

Even knowing that, she wouldn't change a thing. When her father was told he had only months to live, she quit her job to move home and be near him. Those early days in Jackson Hole had been spent at the ranch, doing whatever was needed to ease her mother's burdens and support her father.

Miraculously, the new experimental regime the doctor had tried had vanquished the cancer. Slowly, he'd returned to health. Once he was fully recovered, they hadn't needed her anymore.

Oh, she knew her parents loved having her around. And she loved being close to them and Tripp. The thought of leaving her family held little appeal. For the time being, she'd agreed to take care of some of the business functions involved in running the ranch.

But really, any of the employees could handle the tasks she'd been given. Though Hailey enjoyed the variety of the part-time jobs—and was jazzed about her new venture with Cassidy—the money she brought in wasn't enough to allow her to rent a place of her own.

Once her dad was well, the thought of being twenty-seven and still living with Mom and Dad was untenable. When she'd mentioned she might move back to Denver, her parents insisted she could help them out by moving into their condo in Jackson.

The two-bedroom condo had been initially purchased because her mom wanted to be close to the hospital during the months her father was most ill and receiving treatment. They hadn't yet decided if they were going to sell or rent it out.

Though her mom and dad had made it clear they'd support her in whatever she decided to do, they urged her to stay at least until Tripp and Anna's baby was born.

Hailey had moved into the unit within spitting distance

of Snow King three months ago. She adored having her own place. But it wasn't hers, not really. Despite her parents' insistence that she was doing them a favor, Hailey still felt a bit like a freeloader.

In many ways, Winn's offer had been an answer to her prayers. She could help Winn. She could help Cam. She could make a difference. And, bonus, earn some cash.

"He says he's having fun and wants to stay and play longer," Winn said in satisfaction as he rejoined her. The wonder in his voice touched her.

"Cam will be okay." Hailey placed her hand against his arm. "I have a good feeling."

Winn's slow smile did strange things to her insides. "You know," he said, "I've got a good feeling, too."

Winn had just finished his second cup of morning coffee when a knock sounded. He stiffened when he opened the door and saw the dog at Hailey's side. But, remembering the way Cam's eyes lit up whenever Bandit was near, he smiled and motioned Hailey—and the animal—inside.

"Cam is still sleeping." Winn kept his voice low. "He had a rough night."

Winn had high hopes when they'd returned home after the reception. Cam had been relaxed and happy on the drive home. Once in bed, he'd fallen asleep easily.

But less than an hour later, Cam had awakened, crying. Neither of them had ended up getting much sleep. Seeing tears run down his little boy's cheeks had been like a knife to the heart.

Thankfully, the sympathetic look in Hailey's eyes told Winn he didn't need to go into detail. When she and Bandit drew close, he inhaled the fresh scent of pear. The fruit had always been a favorite of his.

"You look nice." Hailey looked him up and down, her gaze assessing. "Very *GQ*."

Winn felt overdressed in his dark suit, crisp white shirt

and blue patterned tie. Especially when he compared his attire to Hailey's worn jeans and boldly patterned shirt in vivid shades of blues, greens and yellows.

The outfit reminded him of something a college coed on her way to class would wear. Of course, she wasn't a college student. While she was seven years his junior, at twenty-seven, he'd hardly be robbing the cradle if they ever did hook up.

Hook up?

Hailey was his neighbor and friend. If he took her to bed and things went south between them, he might lose her friendship. That risk he wasn't willing to take.

Still, he couldn't help noticing the snug fit of her jeans and the way the shirt outlined her full breasts. Winn forced his attention to the black Hublot on his wrist, checking the time. "I have meetings all morning, but if it's important you can reach me on my cell."

"Got it." Hailey's lips quirked. "Don't call unless Cam is bleeding."

"It's also okay to call if *you're* the one bleeding."

She emitted a laugh, a low and pleasant sound that brought a smile to his lips.

He placed a hand on her bare arm, finding her skin warm and soft as silk. "Seriously. Don't hesitate."

"Aye, aye, Captain." Hailey's mock salute dislodged his hand.

Before he could offer a glib response, she sobered. "You mentioned it was a rough night. Nightmares again?"

"How about I catch you up over a cup of coffee?"

"I love you, Winn Ferris."

He chuckled. "Are you sure it's not my coffee you love?"

She brought a finger to her lips. "That may, just may, be part of it."

"I have a breakfast blend. Or, if you prefer, something called chocolate-glazed donut. The coffee flavor," he clarified at the sudden flash in her eyes. "Not the pastry."

"I'd love a cup of chocolate-glazed donut."

Winn couldn't stop the pained look.

Hailey grinned and followed him into the kitchen, Bandit at her heels. She took a seat at the table. "If you don't like it, why buy it?"

"It came in a variety pack." He shrugged. "I keep it for guests."

"Well, this guest thanks you."

"You'd better taste it first," he warned.

Less than a minute later she sipped the steaming brew, enhanced with a generous helping of half-and-half, and exhaled in pleasure. "This is almost as good as a glazed donut."

"You're easy to please."

She smiled and took another sip.

Winn curled his fingers around his own mug, wishing he didn't have to rush off in a few minutes.

Two lines of worry appeared between Hailey's brows. "Tell me about the nightmares."

"Same as before." Winn sat down his cup, overwhelmed by the depth of his son's pain. "He woke up crying and calling for his mother."

Winn thought of those days and months after his mother's death. Although they hadn't been particularly close—she'd been too busy with her social engagements to give him much time—he'd grieved alone as his father had immediately returned to his demanding schedule.

That would not happen with Cam. His son, not the job, came first.

Hailey gazed down into her coffee, her face filled with sympathy. "Poor little guy."

Winn's throat constricted. He hated that Cam had to go through this. But not *alone,* Winn reminded himself. He took another sip of coffee then stood.

"Will you be home for lunch?" Hailey pushed back her

chair and rose, startling Bandit. The dog shifted his gaze from her to Winn, then dropped back to lie on the floor.

"My mother gave me a recipe for her macaroni and cheese." Hailey walked with Winn to the door. "I've been dying for a chance to make it. It's a lot of carbs but it's fantastic."

Winn couldn't remember the last time anyone—other than a paid staff member—had cooked him a meal. "You don't have to go to all that trouble."

"No trouble," she said cheerfully.

"I should be back by noon." He reached for the doorknob.

Hailey grabbed his arm. "Not so fast."

Winn lifted an eyebrow.

"Your tie is a little crooked." She reached up and adjusted the knot. "Don't worry. I know what I'm doing. I'm always fixing my father's."

"Are you saying I'm like your dad?" Winn found the thought more than a little disturbing.

She grinned impishly. "In the sense you're both smart and charming men, you are. But believe me, Winn, when I look at you, I don't think of my dad."

Winn didn't think. He reached out, pulled her to him and planted a hard kiss on her mouth. "Glad to hear it."

When he reached the bottom of the outside steps, Winn paused, bewildered by what had just occurred. Kissing Hailey had been an impulsive response to a pretty woman's bright smile and teasing words. He never expected it to be so…amazing.

Or to already be wishing he could do it again.

Chapter Eight

In the waning hours of the afternoon, Hailey sat with her mother at the kitchen table she remembered so well from her childhood. Thoughts of the confidences she and her mom had shared at this table over the years brought with it the temptation to confide in her mother once again.

She feared she was falling for Winn. But the feelings were so new, so private, that she couldn't push the words past her lips.

She wasn't at all certain how Winn felt about her. Would she make a fool of herself once again? Would she discover she was only a means to an end for him? When Winn had arrived home for lunch, he'd acted as if the kiss that morning had never happened.

"Both Winn and Cam loved your macaroni and cheese," Hailey said instead. In her family, food was always a popular topic.

While waiting for her mother to reply, Hailey picked up a potato and began to peel it. Though tonight's dinner was in the slow cooker, her mother was already planning tomorrow's menu: potato and leek soup with grilled salmon flaked on it.

"Any accolades are yours." Kathy's eyes glowed with pride. "You were the cook."

A slender woman with dark blond hair cut in a stylish bob, Kathy Randall could easily pass for ten years younger than her fifty-nine years. Recalling Winn's stories about his less-than-loving parents, Hailey felt blessed to have grown up in such a supportive home.

"I'm glad you're teaching me to cook," Hailey blurted out.

Her mother placed her knife on the table and smiled. "I'm happy you're finally interested. Even a year ago you weren't."

"Someday I'll have a family of my own. Preparing meals will be a necessity." Hailey had always assumed she'd one day marry and have a family. She'd thought it would have happened by now. No worries. She had plenty of time. "Regardless, I find I eat healthier when I cook."

Her mother nodded agreement. They worked in companionable silence, finishing with one potato, picking up another. Then her mother's gaze met hers.

"Josh wasn't good enough for you. You're better off without him."

Hailey had expected her humiliating experience with Josh to be brought up sooner or later. She appreciated that her mother had brought him up when they were alone. Both her dad and Tripp were protective of the women in their lives. They'd been furious at Josh's subterfuge.

"Using me to get close to Tripp was bad enough. Discovering he already had a girlfriend…" Hailey exhaled a heavy sigh.

Two lines of worry formed between Kathy's brows. "I hope you won't let your experience with him bias you against other men. There are still good guys out there."

An image of Winn Ferris flashed before her. A good guy? Um, sure. Hailey was *almost* positive if Winn was a cowboy he'd wear a white hat. Then again, he looked really good in black.

"Is there anyone in Jackson Hole you might be interested in dating?"

Despite her mother's casual tone, Hailey wasn't fooled. This was a fishing expedition. She lifted one shoulder in a slight shrug. "I don't think it's wise to start a relationship with someone who lives here. Not until I decide if I'm going to remain in Jackson Hole permanently."

Kathy opened her mouth, but appeared to think for a minute before she spoke. "Remaining here, of course, has to be your decision."

While it might be Hailey's decision, she knew her mother would continue to do everything in her power to entice her to stay. Kathy loved having her daughter back in Wyoming. The truth was, Hailey appreciated Jackson Hole far more than she had when she was young. Back then, she couldn't get out of town quick enough. But her time away had taught her that big cities, while exciting, could also be lonely places.

"Just for the record, I don't agree you should put your social life on hold." Her mother removed the knife and potato from Hailey's fingers then reached across the table and took her hands. "You're a beautiful, intelligent, vibrant young woman. You should be going out and having fun."

"I have fun," Hailey protested. "Cassidy and I went to a movie last week."

There was more Hailey could tell her. Lots more. She'd gone shopping for maternity clothes with Anna. She'd had dinner with an old friend from high-school days. But her mom wasn't talking about fun with friends and family. She wanted Hailey to find someone special, like the man she'd found forty years earlier.

"You've been spending a lot of time with Winn."

Ah, Hailey thought, now they'd reached the heart of the matter.

"I watch Cam during the day." Hailey kept her tone offhand, wondering why she was being forced to point out the obvious. "I'm off at five and free every weekend."

"Suzanne Duggan mentioned she saw you with Winn and his son at Perfect Pizza earlier this week," Kathy said pointedly. "In the evening."

Suzanne, mother of Dr. Tim Duggan, was Kathy's good friend. She was also a woman known for having her finger on the community pulse.

"Winn was hungry for pizza and asked if I wanted to join them for dinner. Because I was also in the mood for pizza, I accepted his invitation. Do you or Suzanne have a problem with that?" There was a challenge in Hailey's softly spoken words, one she was certain her mother caught.

Neither of her parents had seemed particularly happy when she told them she'd agreed to watch Cam for the summer. She wasn't sure if they thought she'd shut the door on other options by taking this on. Or, perhaps, it was the increased contact with Winn that worried them.

"Cam seems like a wonderful child." Her mother spoke slowly, appearing to choose her words carefully. "Your father certainly took right to him."

Since Winn had a lengthy conference call planned for the afternoon and Hailey had errands to run, she and Cam left the condo right after lunch. Once the errands were completed, she'd decided to pay her parents a visit.

When they'd driven up, her dad had been getting into the rusty red pickup he'd purchased new when Bon Jovi topped the rock charts. After a few minutes of getting acquainted, he'd asked Cam if he wanted to help him check on the cattle.

When her dad had plopped his cowboy hat on the boy's head, Cam had hopped into the truck with Bandit on his heels and grinned as if Santa had come down the chimney.

"That's the best thing about watching a child that age." Hailey spoke quickly, eager to make her mother understand that watching Cam was a pleasure, not a chore. "Cameron is a great kid. He's content playing at home with his toy soldiers. But he also likes to hop in the car and go places. He was all for making the trip out here. Especially when I told him Bandit could come along."

"I imagine Winn was relieved to have the place to himself." Kathy's voice cut precisely through the air.

"Actually, we could have stayed as long as we kept the noise down. Or, I could have taken Cam to my place."

"It seems to me it'd be easier if Winn simply allowed you to watch the boy at your place." A hint of censure laced her mother's tone.

"We discussed that option." Hailey turned the unpeeled potato in her hand. "But Winn wants Cam to become familiar with his condo, and to begin to think of it as home."

Kathy raised a skeptical brow.

"I know you don't like Winn—"

"Wherever did you get that idea?" Kathy gave a little laugh, refusing to meet Hailey's gaze. She busied herself inspecting the potatoes.

"You haven't liked him since he went after Anna while Tripp was on the fence."

"Your brother was never on the fence." Her mother's voice rose. "Not when it came to Anna."

Hailey had hit a nerve and they both knew it. Still, she said nothing. She began to peel the potato with slow, deliberate movements.

"Perhaps Tripp was slow to pursue Anna," Kathy admitted after several long seconds had passed. "It wasn't because he didn't care. After what happened to Gayle, I think he was scared to love again."

"Winn didn't do anything wrong by flirting with Anna," Hailey insisted.

"He knew Tripp liked Anna, yet he made a play for her."

Kathy's lips thinned. "I've heard your Mr. Ferris considers a woman available unless she has a ring on her finger."

"First off, he's not my…anything." Hailey waved a hand, ignoring the little pinch to her heart the words engendered. "Second, technically a woman *is* available unless there's a ring on her finger. And last, it's not fair to judge a man on such little evidence. Trust me. Winn's a nice guy."

"I suppose I can give him the benefit of the doubt," was all her mother said and shifted the conversation to dinner.

Tonight her parents would feast on pot roast with new potatoes, carrots, cabbage and baking-powder biscuits. The savory combination was her father's favorite meal.

Hailey's stomach emitted a little growl as the delicious aroma of perfectly spiced beef wafted through the house.

Hearing the sound, Kathy smiled. "Would Winn mind if you and Cam stayed for dinner?"

Hailey thought for a moment. "I'm not sure. He likes to spend as much time with Cam as he can."

"It seems odd he's so concerned now, considering he hadn't seen the child in years."

"That was because of Cam's mother, Vanessa. She—"

The back screen door swung open with a bang. Seconds later Hailey's dad, along with Cam and Bandit, burst into the kitchen.

"Something smells good." Frank bent over and gave his wife a quick kiss before he flashed a smile in his daughter's direction.

"How'd it go?" Hailey kept her tone low, casting a glance at Cam, who stood intently watching Bandit drink from a large water bowl.

Frank clapped a hand on the child's back, startling him. "The cattle were mighty glad to see us. Weren't they, boy?"

Cam looked up. "Th-they came up t-to the truck. B-but I wasn't scared."

"Boy was a big help."

Hailey heard the approval in her father's voice and knew from the child's flush of pleasure that Cam caught it, too.

"I need to make a couple quick calls about some supplies then I'll wash up for dinner." Frank abruptly left the room, turning down the hall leading to his home office.

Cam scuffed the toe of his sneaker into the floor, looking forlorn now that the rangy man with the weathered face and salt-and-pepper hair had left.

Pushing back her chair, Hailey rose and gave Cam a conspiratorial smile. "I know it isn't usually a good idea to eat sweets before a meal. But my mom made chocolate-chip cookies this morning. I'm dying to have one."

Cam's eyes brightened. "I like cookies."

Though her mother had never been a fan of eating between meals, Kathy sighed and grabbed the jar from the counter.

"It's a cookie pig," her mother told Cam. "He loves cookies."

The child studied the jar shaped like a fat pink pig for several seconds. When she removed the lid, Cam reached inside and grabbed one. "Thank you."

Kathy smiled and tousled his hair. "You're very welcome."

While her mother was still in the giving spirit—and before she put the pig's head back on—Hailey snatched one.

"Oh, what the heck." Kathy took one for herself before turning to the refrigerator to get Cam a glass of milk.

Cam gazed down at the cookie. "Grandma Jan made cookies with M&M's."

Hailey paused, curious. *Grandma* Jan?

Once Cam had his milk and they were all seated at the table, Hailey broke off a piece of cookie and spoke in a conversational tone. "Where does Grandma Jan live?"

"With Grandpa Larry." Cam chomped into the cookie.

Kathy stifled a laugh behind a cough. "I believe Hailey was asking what town they lived in."

"In Dunwoody. On Meadowcreek Drive. I know the phone number," the boy said eagerly. "Want me to tell you?"

Hailey shook her head. As she'd had a sorority sister who'd grown up there, she recognized the name of the affluent suburb north of Atlanta. Were these the same grandparents who'd cared for Cam after his mother's death? The ones who'd been so reluctant to turn the boy over to Winn?

"Grandpa Larry used to take me fishing." Cam's expression grew wistful. "Grandma Jan was teaching me how to play the piano."

This was the most the boy had spoken—and without hesitation—since Hailey had met him. "Are Larry and Jan your mommy's mom and dad?"

"No."

Hailey's blood froze at the sharp response. Recognizing Winn's voice, she turned slowly. She'd been so engrossed in the conversation that she hadn't heard a knock at the door or the sound of a single footstep in the hall.

She glanced at her father. He must have let Winn inside. Hailey resisted the urge to shoot him a chiding look. The least he could have done was given some kind of warning that they had company.

Winn followed her father into the room, looking mouth-wateringly good in navy pants and a thinly striped cotton shirt.

Hailey's cheeks burned. Dear God, she hoped Winn wouldn't think she'd been pumping Cam for information. What was he doing here, anyway? He'd told her the conference call would go right up to five o'clock.

Glancing at the clock, Hailey winced. Nearly six. She pulled to her feet. "I'm sorry. I lost track of time. But you didn't need to drive all the way out here. I'd have brought him home."

"I was in the area."

It was a lie. It had to be. What business could Winn

have way out here? And why hadn't he simply called or texted her?

Winn turned to Cam. "Ready to go, sport?"

The boy shook his head. "I haven't finished my cookie."

"Cookie?"

Hailey stifled a groan.

The boy held up half of the cookie he had left for his father's inspection. "It's l-like the ones Grandma Jan makes. It's real g-good."

A muscle in Winn's jaw jumped.

Hailey opened her mouth to tell Winn that she'd been the one to offer the treat so close to suppertime. If he was going to be angry at anyone, it should be her.

Winn offered his son an easy smile. "Chocolate-chip cookies are my favorite."

It wasn't at all what Hailey expected him to say.

Cam turned to Hailey's mom. "My daddy likes cookies. C-can he have one, too?"

Winn stilled, a light flaring in those hazel eyes.

Hailey's heart thumped unevenly. As far as she knew, this was the first time since arriving in Jackson Hole that Cam had referred to Winn as his "daddy."

"I—I—" This time it was the normally loquacious Winn Ferris who stuttered.

"Of course he can have a cookie." Hailey hurriedly retrieved the pig from the counter.

Cam had moved to his father's side and was tugging on his sleeve.

"It's a cookie pig." The boy spoke in a loud whisper. "He loves to eat cookies. Just like you and me."

Hailey held out the jar and tried not to smile.

"Thanks." Winn absently took a cookie then glanced around the room as if taking everything in: the bowl of peeled potatoes on the table, the slow cooker on the counter and the pie cooling on a rack.

Hailey saw the kitchen through his eyes. The room radiated warmth, home and love.

A half smile lifted Winn's lips before he placed a hand on Cam's shoulder. "Time we get going."

"If you don't have plans for dinner—" Kathy spoke hurriedly as Cam's face took on a mulish expression "—we'd love for you to join us. It's nothing fancy—"

"Just the best pot roast west of the Mississippi," Frank interjected, speaking for the first time since he and Winn had entered the kitchen. "Stay. Try it. You'll agree I'm right."

Whether it was the simple fact that it was dinnertime, or the pleading look on Cam's face that made Winn agree, Hailey didn't know.

She only knew she was glad Winn had decided to stay. Hailey had a burning need to get to know him better. And no one—other than perhaps Suzanne Duggan—beat her mother for ferreting out information.

Especially when it came to someone she worried was becoming an important part of her daughter's life.

Chapter Nine

If Winn would have been the kind of man to lean back in a chair and rub his belly, this would have been the time.

Frank had been right. Winn had enjoyed many meals at five-star restaurants. This one ranked up there with the best of them.

As if he could read Winn's mind, Frank grinned. "I told you."

Winn shifted his gaze to Kathy. "Excellent meal, Mrs. Randall."

"Coming from someone who frequents nice restaurants, that's high praise." Kathy's cheeks pinked. "And please, call me Kathy."

During the meal Kathy had attempted several times to steer the conversation around to Winn's personal life, but her husband had blocked her efforts. Frank, a former board of trustees member, had a keen interest in land development and ecosystems. He'd found an expert on those topics in Winn.

Frank kept a spirited discussion going for most of the

meal. They were almost finished eating when Frank lifted his wineglass and ceded the conversational ball to his wife.

"So, Winn." Kathy's eyes were assessing. "You're about Tripp's age, I think."

Though it was more statement than question, it seemed to require a response. Winn lifted his own glass of wine, catching an apologetic gleam in Frank's eyes.

Let the inquisition begin....

"I believe so," Winn said in an amiable tone that he didn't need to force. After such a delicious meal, it was hard to get too worked up about anything, especially such a basic question.

"Most men, when they reach your age, have married or been involved in one or two serious relationships."

There was a question in there somewhere. Winn leaned back in his chair. He'd wondered how much Hailey had shared with her family about his relationship with Vanessa. Apparently nothing at all.

He smiled and shot a warm smile in Hailey's direction.

"Have you ever been married, Winn?" Frank asked.

Before Winn had a chance to respond, Bandit growled low in his throat. There was a distant sound of the front door opening.

Bandit barked just as a masculine voice called out, "It's just us."

Cam looked up from the biscuit he'd been crumbling on his plate, his eyes alert and curious. "Who's here?"

"My brother," Hailey said with a smile. "And his wife."

Kathy pushed back from the table and hurried from the room.

"We're in the dining room," Frank called out.

Kathy returned with Tripp and her daughter-in-law, Anna.

Considered by many to be one of the most beautiful women in Jackson Hole, Anna glided into the room on three-inch heels. Her green dress draped her figure in such a way that if Winn hadn't known she was pregnant he'd never have guessed.

When he'd first arrived in town, Winn had been mesmerized by her sultry good looks. But his taste had changed. He found he now preferred blondes who radiated an abundance of girl-next-door charm.

"We knew we'd interrupt your supper," Anna was saying to Kathy as she entered the kitchen, "but we were so excited and—"

She stopped suddenly as she caught sight of Winn and Cam seated with the family around the large oval table.

Winn rose to his feet. "Hello, Anna. Tripp."

"Nice to see you, Ferris." Tripp stepped over to shake his hand then shot a curious glance at the boy. "And this is…?"

"My son, Cameron." Winn performed brief introductions.

Hailey rose to give her sister-in-law a quick hug. "You look fabulous. I can't wait to hear what has the two of you so excited."

"It can wait." Anna paused, a legal-size manila envelope clutched in her hand. "I didn't realize you had company."

"Not company." Hailey waved a dismissive hand. "Just Winn and Cam."

Still, Anna hesitated, shifting uncertainly from one foot to the other.

"Actually, we were getting ready to leave," Winn said smoothly. "Time to go, Cameron."

"B-but M-Mrs. Randall said she had apple p-p-pie for d-dessert."

Anna shifted her gaze to the boy, offering him a dazzling smile. "Apple pie? Do you think she'll let me have a piece?"

"Y-you c-could ask her," Cam stammered.

If she noticed the stutter, Anna gave no indication. "Good idea."

Anna shifted her gaze to her mother-in-law.

"We have pie enough for everyone," Kathy said immediately.

"Thank you for the wonderful meal." Winn motioned for Cam to get up, ignoring his son's protest.

"Please don't leave on our account." Anna placed a hand on his arm.

"I—I want p-pie," Cam whined.

"Stay," Hailey mouthed from across the table.

"No need for the two of you to run off," Frank added.

Winn realized he was on the verge of causing a scene. He decided to eat quickly then leave. "We'll stay for dessert."

"Yippee." Cameron high-fived Hailey.

"Never pegged you for a family man," Tripp commented as the women busied themselves clearing the table, brushing aside all offers to help.

"I never pegged me for one, either," Winn said with a rueful smile, recalling how shocked he'd been when he learned Vanessa was pregnant. "That changed when Cam was born…"

Tripp nodded. A look of understanding filled his eyes.

For the first time, Winn felt a connection with the man. Not one forged over a boardroom table, but arising out of a common understanding of what really mattered in life.

"Mom is bringing the pie." Hailey entered the dining room and placed a tray holding a carafe of coffee and cups and saucers on the table.

Hailey informed them, with a special glance toward Anna—who'd rejoined the group—that the coffee was a special decaffeinated blend from Hill of Beans. The pie ended up being caramel apple with a dollop of real whipped cream on top.

Halfway through dessert, Anna apparently grew impatient and opened the envelope.

Frank cocked his head and stared at the black-and-gray pictures. "What is it?"

"It's the ultrasound of our grandbaby." Kathy breathed the words, her voice thick with emotion.

In his business, Winn had perfected the art of reading beneath a man's carefully composed facade. Tripp sat directly across from him, giving Winn a good view of his face. There was excitement and pride in Tripp's eyes, but also worry. Completely understandable considering his first wife's death had been due to late-pregnancy complications.

Kathy stared hard at the image, then pointed with one finger. "Is that a—"

"Our baby is a boy." Anna reached out and grasped her husband's hand. "He's absolutely perfect and just where he should be development-wise."

"And you?" Frank cleared his throat, looking nearly as worried as his son. "How are you doing, Anna?"

"All good." She may have spoken to her father-in-law, but her reassuring gaze remained on her husband. "Healthy as a horse."

"I want to see the baby pictures." Cam scampered around the table. His eyes widened as he stared at the black-and-white photo. Cam shifted his gaze to his dad, confusion blanketing his face. "That's not a baby."

"That's what a baby looks like before it's born," Winn told his son.

Cam glanced at the picture one more time before returning to the table to finish his pie.

Hailey rose to lean over her mother's shoulder for a better look. "What a handsome boy."

Winn caught Tripp's gaze. "Congratulations."

"Thanks."

Frank clapped a hand on his son's shoulder. "It'll all be okay."

This time. Though the words remained unsaid, Winn heard them clearly.

"I know, Dad." Tripp told his father. "I know it will."

The talk shifted to babies, then to stories about Tripp and Hailey growing up.

"From a young age Tripp always knew ranching wasn't for him," Frank said equitably, not appearing bothered by the idea. "His studies were his focus. Hailey, on the other hand, was always more focused on *social* studies."

Everyone laughed. Winn wondered if he was the only one who noticed Hailey's smile didn't quite meet her eyes.

The momentary lull that settled over the table was broken by Cam's declaration that this was the "bestest" pie he'd ever eaten.

Kathy beamed at the pronouncement, a fact for which Winn was grateful. When he was growing up, use of incorrect grammar had been grounds for immediate and harsh punishment.

His father saw any faux pas as reflecting poorly on himself. Looking at Cam's sweet face, all Winn saw was a young boy offering a heartfelt compliment.

"Mary Karen and Travis are hosting their annual summer solstice party on the twenty-first." Anna's lips curved. "I wonder if there will be mistletoe this year."

"Mistletoe?" Frank's brows pulled together. "In June?"

"It's practically a tradition," Hailey explained. "You can't go to a party at their home without encountering mistletoe."

"Sounds like great fun." Kathy shot her husband a suggestive glance. "Should I see if I can wrangle an invitation, Frank?"

"Don't do it," Tripp warned, his arm resting on the back of his wife's chair. "You never know what you might see there. Or what kinds of games will be played."

Frank put down his coffee cup. "Now I'm intrigued."

"Hailey can tell you all about the games. She played Spin the Bottle with Winn," Tripp announced, "the first night they met."

Tripp gave a loud *oof* when Hailey's foot connected

with his skin. "Hey. At least I know the names of all the girls I kiss. *Used* to kiss," Tripp amended when his wife lifted a brow.

Frank leveled a look at his daughter. "Hailey Anne. Please don't tell me that you go around kissing men you just met."

"It was mistletoe, Frank," her mother soothed.

"Actually, it wasn't," Hailey said in a breezy tone, an impish gleam in her blue eyes. "Like Big-Mouth said, we were playing Spin the Bottle."

"My goodness." Kathy's hand fluttered in the air. "I didn't know anyone played that game anymore."

"They shouldn't," Frank muttered darkly.

Winn tried to contain his grin.

"Anna and I were playing, too," Tripp offered, earning a grateful glance from his sister. "If that makes you feel better."

"It doesn't," Frank said flatly.

"There were lots of old games being played," Winn repeated, trying to draw the attention off Hailey. "Not just Spin the Bottle."

"Is Spinning the Bottle a fun game?" Cam asked, and Winn suppressed a groan.

"It's a kissing game," Anna explained. "A person spins a bottle on the floor and they have to kiss whoever it points to."

"Yuck." Cam's face scrunched up. He shook his head vigorously. "I'm not playing that game ever."

The adults chuckled and the tension in the room eased. Winn couldn't believe Hailey's parents were getting so worked up over a single kiss.

A kiss he still remembered...

"Since Winn was a stranger, I'm sure it was just a little peck," Kathy reassured her husband.

"Actually, the kiss was so hot it was a wonder we weren't rolling around on the floor." Hailey brought a finger to her lips, her blue eyes twinkling. "At least, that's how I remember it."

Though laughter spilled over again, Winn admitted—but only to himself—that was exactly how he remembered it, too.

Conversation finally drifted to the upcoming Fourth of July celebration.

Winn listened with half an ear, sipping his coffee. While the conversation was now firmly off the kiss, he found that was all he could think about. Not the one Hailey had planted on him at that long-ago party, but the one earlier today.

He didn't regret the impulsive gesture. Hailey's lips had been as sweet as he remembered. When they were alone and she brought it up, he could explain away the gesture by saying it was a thank-you for being so kind to Cam and for all the nice things she'd done. But Winn knew he wouldn't. He'd be lying. Not only to her but to himself.

The truth was, he was attracted to Hailey. He liked her, enjoyed being with her. While he certainly hadn't been looking to become involved with anyone—

"Winn."

He blinked and discovered Hailey crouched by his chair, her hand on his arm.

Winn glanced around and discovered everyone's attention was now focused on Cam, who was proudly putting Bandit through his repertoire of tricks.

"Cam wants to ride home with me," Hailey told Winn in a low voice. "But I need to stop and see Cassidy about an upcoming salon day party."

"No worries," Winn said, slightly puzzled. Didn't she realize she was officially off the clock? "He'll ride with me."

"I know, but—" Two bright patches of pink colored her cheeks. "Cam asked this afternoon if I could read to him before he fell asleep. I'd like to do it, if it's not a problem. I can stop over after I meet with Cassidy."

"You don't need to go to that trouble," Winn said. "I know how to read."

That didn't even coax a smile from her.

"It's no trouble," Hailey spoke quickly. "I want to do it."

He was touched by her caring. "Let's play it by ear. If it works for you, stop by. If not, I'll do it."

"I'll be there."

Winn grinned. "First thing in the morning. Last thing at night. How did I get so lucky?"

"Keep that thought," Hailey said in a teasing tone. "I predict you'll be sick of me before the summer is over."

"I believe the opposite will be true."

A startled look crossed her face and Winn cursed his impulsiveness. She'd just split from that weasel Gratzke. Obviously the last thing on her mind was getting involved with someone else.

"What are you two discussing so intently?" Hailey's mother asked.

Before Winn had a chance to speak, Hailey flashed her parents a saucy smile. "What do you think? We're planning our next kiss."

Chapter Ten

Hailey rapped lightly on Winn's door. Her meeting with Cassidy had taken longer than expected. While she wasn't exactly sure what time eight-year-olds went to bed, the fact that it was almost nine o'clock had her hesitating.

Perhaps she should have texted Winn before knocking. But before she could pull out her phone—or simply slink away—the door opened.

Hailey blinked once. Then again. She'd never seen Winn dressed so casually. Gray running pants. Black T-shirt. Bare feet.

Even as her blood began to hum, she forced a teasing smile. "Who are you and what have you done with Winston Ferris?"

Winn laughed and stepped aside. "Things are pretty low-key around here tonight. Come in."

As she strolled past him, Hailey noticed his dark hair was slightly damp. Instead of the expensive cologne he often wore, she caught a pleasing whiff of soap mixed with shampoo.

"You smell really good." The second the words left her lips, Hailey wished she could pull them back. Sheesh. What was she…fifteen?

"Thanks." Winn acted as if her comment wasn't at all odd. "Cam and I took showers. He has on his pajamas, but I decided I should stay dressed since you were coming over."

Hailey gave a dismissive wave. "Being fully clothed is highly overrated."

"You could take off yours and I could take off mine." His eyes flashed with good humor. "But what would your mother say?"

Hailey leaned close and lowered her voice to a conspiratorial whisper. "I won't tell her if you won't."

He trailed a finger up her arm. "Then let's do it."

For a second, Hailey thought he was serious. Then she saw the irreverent gleam in those hazel eyes. With great effort she reminded herself why she was here.

Hailey stepped back and gestured to the bag slung over her arm. The designer satchel was a vivid royal blue. It had room for everything she needed, as well as the entire state of Wyoming.

Stylish, yet eminently practical, was how she regarded the purse Cassidy teasingly called her "suitcase."

Hailey's hand dived into the bag and emerged with a paperback. "My parents read *The White Mountains* to me when I was around Cam's age."

She lovingly caressed the first volume of The Tripods trilogy with the pads of her fingers. When she looked up, Hailey found Winn staring.

The teasing gleam in his eyes had disappeared. The expression on his face sent blood coursing through her veins like an awakened river. Hailey licked her suddenly dry lips. "Where's Cam?"

"In his room. Playing with his soldiers." Winn pulled his gaze from her lips with visible effort. "You do realize what his first question will be when he sees you."

"That's easy. He'll ask what book I brought."

"Where's Bandit?"

Confused at the abrupt change of subject, Hailey answered cautiously. "Bandit is at home."

"No. That will be Cam's first question." Reaching out, Winn briefly touched a silky lock. "Have I ever told you how much I like your hair? It's the most beautiful shade of gold."

Though he lowered his hand, the air between them pulsated with need. For one, two, three hard beats, Hailey stood there as if her feet were rooted in concrete.

Bold, Hailey told herself. *Be bold.*

With her heart still thumping in her chest, Hailey stepped forward, the book clutched in her hand.

"What did you say, Mr. Ferris?" She stared up at him through lowered lashes. "I was so focused on your mouth I missed your words."

"I—" Winn paused as if trying to recall something just out of reach. "I believe I said I want to kiss you. If I didn't, that's what I meant."

Hailey flashed a sly smile. "Great minds obviously think alike."

The heat in his eyes sent a tingle of excitement up her spine. She wound her arms around his neck and lifted her face.

As if unwilling to waste another second, Winn lowered his head. He folded her more fully into his arms, anchoring her against his chest as his mouth covered hers in a deep, compelling kiss.

Dreamily, Hailey stroked his thick hair.

He tasted like spearmint toothpaste, her favorite flavor. His hand rose and cupped her breast, his fingers teasing the nipple into a hardened—

"Hailey!" A boy's joy-filled cry had her jumping back, her breath coming fast.

Dear God, was this how her parents felt all those times she'd walked in on them kissing in the kitchen?

Like a rocket, Cam launched himself at her, wrapping his spindly arms around her waist.

The red, white and blue Captain America pajamas were well-worn and obviously a favorite. Cam's hair was slightly damp with tufts of light brown hair sticking up in patches.

Cam's gaze shifted from his dad to Hailey. "Where's Bandit?"

"Told you," Winn murmured.

"He's at home sleeping on his doggie bed." Hailey reached out and gently smoothed down Cam's hair. "You and my dad wore him out."

Cam chewed on his lower lip. "Bandit ran after the cows. He got in big trouble."

It was the first Hailey had heard of the dog causing problems. She pulled her brows together. Her dad was protective of his prizewinning cattle. "That's not good."

"Bandit was sorry. Really, really sorry," Cam continued in a quick small voice, his bottom lip now trembling. "D-d-don't be mad at him."

Hailey exchanged a glance with Winn, then offered the boy a reassuring smile. "I'm not angry. I do want to make sure Bandit behaves himself in the future so my dad will be happy to see him."

"Bandit came right away when your dad called. He said Bandit was a good boy," Cam told her, his expression earnest. "He said I was a good boy, too."

It was obvious the compliment had meant a lot to the child. Her dad had always been generous with his praise.

"I'm sure he appreciated your company," Hailey assured him. "Feeding cattle is more fun with a good helper."

"I helped Grandpa Larry plant corn once. It grew this tall." Cam raised the hand holding a toy soldier toward the ceiling. "Grandpa Larry said I was a good helper, too."

The smile slipped from Cam's face. "I miss him."

For a second, Hailey thought the tears welling in the boy's eyes might spill over.

Out of the corner of her eye, Hailey noticed Winn's expression had gone stony.

Time to get off this topic. Hailey lifted the book. "Ready for a bedtime story?"

Cam's tears disappeared and curiosity filled his gaze. "What's it about?"

"Aliens," Winn said in a spooky voice usually reserved for Halloween.

"It's about boys, just a little older than you," Hailey said, then added, "They fight aliens."

A light sparked in Cam's eyes. "Do the boys beat the monsters?"

Hailey started to answer, but Winn winked at his son. "We'll have to read the book and find out."

"I like to read." Cam prattled on about his reading prowess all the way to his bedroom. "My teacher, Miss Leininger, said I was one of the best in her class."

"Smart boy." Hailey slanted a sideways glance at Winn. "Like his dad."

Cam seemed surprised that Winn planned to sit down with them. Apparently, only his mommy had ever read him bedtime stories.

Hailey took a seat beside Cam on the bed. Once Winn had settled on the other side of the boy, she began to read. The story about tripods and metal skullcaps quickly transported her to a dystopian future. She reached page five before it hit her that she should give Winn a turn.

Alternating every four or five pages, they quickly reached the end of the first chapter. Still wide awake— and caught up in the story—Cam begged them to continue.

Hailey wasn't sure if it was the pleading or the fact that Cam had crawled onto his lap that caused Winn to agree.

The bedside lamp cast a golden glow over the room.

A warm blanket of contentment settled around Hailey's shoulders as she took her turn reading.

By the time they reached the end of the second chapter, Cam's eyelids began to droop.

Winn planted a kiss atop Cam's head, his eyes filled with such tenderness it made Hailey want to weep. She wished all those who called Winn a cold fish could see him now. Gentle, kind and so full of love for a little boy who wasn't even his flesh and blood.

"Good night, sport." Winn pulled up the covers.

The boy stirred, blinked. "I have to say my prayers first."

To his credit, the momentary flash of surprise in Winn's eyes didn't make it to his face. He watched wordlessly as the thin-framed boy folded his hands, the toy soldier still clasped in small fingers as he began to pray.

"Thank you for letting me ride in the truck and see the cows today. Thank you for my daddy and Hailey and Bandit. Thank you for Grandpa Larry and Grandma Jan." The child paused and when he spoke again, his voice wobbled. "If you see my mommy and daddy in heaven, tell them I miss them. Amen."

Hailey didn't dare look at Winn. She swallowed past the lump in her throat as Cam's eyes fluttered shut.

When the child's breathing grew even and regular, Winn gently tugged the toy soldier from Cam's hand. He placed the infantryman on top of the nightstand.

Hailey didn't speak until they were back in the living room.

"You're a good father." She could have said more, could have told him there was nothing so sexy as a man who was kind to children. But she felt strangely off balance.

It was almost as if she and Winn had turned a corner she hadn't known they'd been approaching. Avoiding his gaze, Hailey lifted her bag then slung it over her shoulder.

"There's no reason for you to rush off."

Something in his voice wrapped itself around her spine

and caused an inward shudder. The air suddenly hummed with electricity and Hailey couldn't move. Not if that step took her away from him.

Hoping she wasn't making a huge mistake, she whirled and shot Winn a flirty smile. "Entice me to stay."

"Merlot?" He raised a brow, a smile lurking in his eyes. "The year 2010 was exceptional in the Bordeaux region."

Hailey had never seen such beautiful eyes. Such compelling eyes. Eyes with the power to weaken her knees when they locked on hers.

Hailey dropped her satchel to the floor. "You had me at Merlot."

He stepped toward her, put his hands on her shoulders. "Sit. Relax." His voice was smooth as the fine bourbon her father drank. "I'll get us a glass."

When he made no move to leave, she thought he was going to kiss her. Her heartbeat hitched. Her lips began to tingle in anticipation. Disappointment flooded her when he abruptly turned and left the room.

Hailey meandered to the window. Too geared up to sit, she opened the blinds and let the gentle rainfall calm her.

After a moment, Winn joined her and handed her a glass of red.

"I love rain." She turned, and the second her eyes touched his, something inside her seemed to lock into place and she couldn't look away. "I—I especially like it when I'm inside all warm and dry. Sipping fine wine with a handsome man is like icing on the cake. I don't know about you, but for me icing is always the best part of anything."

She was babbling, Hailey realized. She clamped her lips together before she started in on the merits of cream cheese versus fluffy white frosting.

Without taking his gaze from hers, Winn cupped her elbow in his hand, maneuvered her to the sofa then sat beside her. "I like the sound of rain, the smell of it. But being with you is the ultimate pleasure."

"Warm and dry?"

"Not necessary." Winn's lips curved. "Getting wet would be an excuse to warm each other up. And *that* I'd like very much."

Warm each other up.

Was he implying he wanted to take her to bed, to be her lover?

Perhaps. Hailey took another sip of Merlot. Unless, of course, this was simply how he flirted and she was reading too much into his words.

Thinking of Josh, Hailey ruefully admitted she didn't have a good record of accurately reading a man's signals. She'd been convinced he liked her when he didn't give a flying fig. Once again, she could be seeing what wasn't there.

Only one way to know for sure…

Impulsively, Hailey turned in her seat and faced Winn. "Do you want to sleep with me?"

His hand jerked back, nearly spilling his wine. "Beg pardon?"

"You heard me." Proud of herself for taking charge of the situation, Hailey sat back. Though her insides jittered like a bowl of gelatin, outwardly she appeared calm. Or so she hoped.

The calm lasted until Winn caught her hand in his, lifted it to his mouth and pressed a kiss in the palm. "First, let me say that I knew you were special from the moment we met."

The words reached inside her to soothe a raw, tender place. She'd never considered herself to be all that special. Everyone knew—and she accepted—that her brother was the smart one in the family, the successful one.

"The bottle lands on me," Winn continued, his gaze dark and smoldering. "I expect a peck on the cheek. Instead, I get a kiss that launches my heart into the stratosphere."

So, she hadn't been the only one who'd felt the punch of that first kiss and been startled by it. Despite the alarming rush of sheer physical awareness that had assailed her as soon as she'd set eyes on him, she'd been shocked by the force of her desire for a man whose name she hadn't known.

"Your boldness was as appealing as the kiss." Winn's lips curved, admiration in his eyes. "You're a treasure."

A treasure.

A chill snaked up her spine, dousing the heat. Josh had used nearly the same words when telling her how much she'd meant to him. Lies. All lies.

Well, Hailey wasn't interested in being someone's treasure. Maybe she'd yearned for that once upon a time. Perhaps, eventually, she'd take a chance and trust again. But not now. Not so soon after being played for a fool.

She didn't want the burden of worrying if Winn was sincere. And she wouldn't have to worry. Not if the only thing she was in the market for was fun and companionship.

"Yes or no, Ferris." Thankfully, the words came out light and teasing, just as she intended.

"Hailey, darling, I've wanted you in my bed even before that first kiss." He ran a finger up her arm, leaving a trail of heat in its wake. "But I'm not convinced this is the best time for either of us to begin a relationship."

"Who said anything about a relationship?"

Surprise flickered in his hazel eyes before the shutters dropped. Several long seconds passed.

"I've a feeling one night with you wouldn't be enough." There was regret and some other emotion Hailey couldn't identify in the words.

"I don't think it'd be enough for me, either." Hailey forced a chuckle past the tightness in her throat. "I'm not in the market for happily-ever-after, Winn. Just for happily-right-now."

There appeared to be an inner war raging in his eyes. He said nothing for so long, she was tempted to snatch up her bag and head for the door. Then his arm tightened around her shoulder. "Stay the night."

"Tonight?" Hailey couldn't hide her surprise.

"No. Twenty years from now," he said with a laugh.

"I want to, I really do." Hailey blew out a ragged breath. "But I can't. Not with a child in the next room."

"*In the next room* being the key phrase," Winn said pointedly.

Hailey was well aware couples didn't give up sex just because they had a child. Her birth six years after her brother was proof of that fact. But she wasn't Winn's wife.

While she had no problem having a fling with him, Hailey shared her parents' belief that single men or women shouldn't have sex while children were in the house. The sentiment was too deeply ingrained for her to ignore, no matter how tempted she was to play the "just this once" card.

"I can't," she said, winning the internal battle. "Not with Cam here."

A smile slipped from Winn's lips and she sensed his frustration. "Cam isn't going anywhere. If not now, when?"

"Sometime when he's spending the night with a friend or gone for a playdate in the afternoon." She placed her palm against Winn's cheek. "I want you too much not to make it happen. We just have to be patient and wait for the perfect time."

"The perfect time," Winn muttered to himself an hour later. He stared at the empty bottle of wine and listened to rain pelt the windows.

Thankfully, Hailey's reluctance hadn't extended to make-out sessions on the sofa. They'd spent a half hour kissing like two teenagers in the throes of youthful passion before she'd pulled from his arms, her breath coming in short puffs.

After buttoning her shirt, she'd left, leaving him confused and too frustrated to sleep.

From the instant he'd seen the pretty blonde, he'd been

drawn to her. The kisses they'd shared only whetted his appetite for more. But the attraction wasn't only physical.

Winn admired the woman behind the thousand-watt smile. With her, he could be himself. But once again, a woman he genuinely liked didn't want him. Except in bed.

He grimaced, wondering when a good romp between the sheets had ceased being enough. The truth was, he'd grown weary of dating around. He was thirty-four, for chrissakes. He wanted more. He wanted Hailey Randall.

Not just in his bed but in his life. He didn't want a casual fling. He wanted to build a relationship with her and see where it took them. He wanted to put down roots. But with her "happily-right-now" comment, she'd made it clear she wasn't looking for more. At least not with him.

He'd sleep with her; that was a foregone conclusion. Winn leaned back against the plush leather cushions of his sofa and stared unseeing at the muted big screen. He'd keep it light and fun. For now.

Eventually something would have to change.

He wanted more for himself and certainly more for Cam. *Cam.*

Was his son the reason Hailey couldn't see herself in a serious relationship with him? Did she not want a man with a child?

Winn tightened his jaw. If that was the reason, it was best they keep it light.

Because any woman who wanted to be part of his life would have to understand that he and Cam were a package deal.

He wasn't giving up his son again.

Chapter Eleven

The week flew by. Finally it was the weekend and time to par-tay. Hailey smiled into the mirror then grimaced. What a pretty picture she'd almost made. Red jersey top. Black skinny knit pants. Cherry lipstick on her teeth. She leaned forward and rubbed the unwanted smidge of color off with her finger.

Hailey flashed another bright smile, her eyes sharp and assessing. Sparkling white with no trace of red. Satisfied, she stepped back and smoothed a hand over her fluttering stomach.

Why had she told Winn she wanted to sleep with him? More importantly, why had he let all these days pass without making a move?

Granted, he'd been busy brokering golf-course development deals all week. Any free time had been spent with Cam. Hailey had been included in several of their outings. Though, when Winn had taken Cam to Kate Dennes, the two had gone to the pediatrician alone.

Hailey understood. After all, it wasn't as if she was part of the family.

A knock on the door had her checking her teeth one last time before hurrying to answer it. The sole agenda for the evening was Mary Karen and Travis's annual summer solstice party. Since she and Winn had both planned to attend, he'd invited her to ride with him and Cam.

Following past tradition, Mary Karen had hired several high-school girls and boys to watch the children of party attendees. Cam was excited that many of his new friends would be there.

Hailey opened her front door in time to hear Cam say worriedly, "Maybe she isn't here."

"I'm home." She motioned them both inside. "And I'm almost ready. I just need to put on my shoes."

She plopped down onto the nearest chair and grabbed her new sparkly red Dorothy shoes from the floor. Flats might be more appropriate for a casual summer party, but she'd been looking for an excuse to wear the glittery heels.

She lifted her gaze to find Winn staring. Cam had crossed the room to rub Bandit's belly while the collie sprawled on his back and thumped his tail.

"You look incredible," Winn murmured.

Hailey's heart fluttered. "You don't look half-bad yourself."

She gave his lean, muscular body another once-over. Dark trousers. Black knit shirt. Italian loafers. Forget business casual. Winn had *sexy* casual down to an art form.

Tall. Dark. Delicious.

She shivered as the ache of wanting returned. Six days since she'd proposed a fling. Six nights spent alone, wondering when the clock would chime announcing the perfect time had arrived.

When his gaze met hers, Hailey experienced what could only be described as a premonitory jolt. The clock would strike tonight. The exact time didn't matter. Neither did the specifics. Before the sun rose on another day, she would lie in Winn's arms. The knowledge wrapped the evening in a festive ribbon.

"Daddy says there will be lots of kids at the party." Cam plopped down on the sofa beside Hailey. "Bandit likes kids. But he says Bandit can't come."

Daddy, again.

Hailey offered up a prayer of thanks then focused on the small boy.

"From what I understand, it's usually pretty crowded." She leaned over to stroke the top of the dog's head. "I think Bandit will be more happy at home watching his doggie movie."

"Doggie movie?"

Hailey shifted her gaze to Winn and saw amusement lurking in his eyes.

"The DVD is called *While You're Gone*." Hailey ignored the heat making its way up her neck. Her father had razzed her when she told him about purchasing the video. But, she reminded herself, Frank had grown up on a ranch where animals weren't generally regarded as pets.

Would Winn think it equally silly? She lifted her chin. "It takes the dog on a virtual walk through a forest. All sorts of animals show up. The movie even includes special sounds only a dog can hear."

Cam looked intrigued.

Winn cocked his head but didn't scoff.

"Let me show you." Hailey started the DVD. Sounds of nature mixed with the joyous peals of children's laughter. Bandit's ears shot up and his dark eyes focused intently on the screen.

"I want to stay and watch the movie with Bandit." The mulish expression she'd seen several times this week on Cam's face reappeared.

While Cam was a good-natured kid, he had a stubborn streak. A fact she and Winn had both discovered.

"I'd like to see it, too," Winn said. "Perhaps Hailey can bring the movie over one day this week. We can watch it together."

Cam's eyes widened then narrowed suspiciously. "You'd watch it, too?"

Winn ruffled his son's hair. "Of course. I like nature walks as much as the next guy."

Hailey bit the inside of her cheek to keep from chuckling.

"Mr. Lassiter told me Charlie was looking forward to seeing you tonight," Winn said in a casual tone.

Hailey decided now was the time to add her voice to the effort. She turned to Winn. "Did Dr. Fisher tell you they have a huge train set up in the lower level of their house?"

"No," Winn said, playing along. "I hadn't heard anything about a train."

Like a child in a classroom, Cam waved his hand wildly in the air.

"Cam," Hailey called on him.

"I know all about it. Charlie and me and Logan are going to play with the train," Cam told them.

"Sounds like we better get on the road," Winn said mildly. "We wouldn't want to keep Charlie and Logan waiting."

Cam glanced at Bandit. The dog seemed mesmerized by the virtual game of fetch playing on the screen.

"Logan said the train blows real smoke," Cam told them as they headed to the car.

"Cool," Winn said.

Hailey kept her expression impassive, wondering if, like her, Winn had noticed Cam wasn't stammering tonight. At least for the moment.

One glance at the smile on his lips gave her the answer.

On the way to the Fishers' home in the mountains, Cam talked continuously, barely stuttering at all. Hailey wondered if some of the speech-therapy "games" they'd been playing were having a positive effect. Or perhaps Cam was becoming more relaxed and comfortable with his new life in Jackson Hole.

Though Hailey was fairly certain the boy had told his dad about his playdate earlier in the week with Charlie Lassiter, Cam recounted the day in vivid detail.

"Hailey made us hot dogs for lunch," the boy told Winn. "We wanted chips but we had oranges instead."

"When I was a boy, my father never let me have hot dogs," Winn said with a rueful smile, his gaze fixed on the road.

Cam's small brows pulled together in a frown. "Your dad s-sounds m-mean."

"Not mean. He just has an aversion to processed meats." To Winn's credit, he didn't trash Jim. Obviously he didn't want to prejudice the boy against the "grandfather" he'd soon meet. Winn's father had been out of town for almost a week but was due back tomorrow.

"I still think he s-sounds mean," Cam insisted.

"We're going to his ranch tomorrow," Winn said in a casual tone. "You'll get a chance to meet him. As well as his housekeeper, Elena."

"She's a real sweetie," Hailey told Cam.

Looking dubious, Cam shrugged. He lifted the iPad from his lap and began to play a game involving a "shiver" of sharks.

"Will this be the first time Cam and your father have met?" Hailey asked in a low voice as Winn turned onto the mountain road leading to the Fisher home.

"Dad saw him several times when I shared joint custody with…" Winn paused as if concerned about his son overhearing. "I don't believe Cam remembers those encounters."

Hailey thought of Jim Ferris's acerbic wit and Cam's tender spirit. The fierce feeling of protectiveness that rose inside Hailey surprised her with its intensity. The speech therapist in her was concerned that a blunt comment or two from Jim could set Cam's progress back. But mostly she was concerned about the little boy's heart. She felt like a mother lion poised to defend one of her cubs.

"Aren't you worried?" The question popped out before Hailey could remind herself that Cam wasn't her cub, er, child, and where Winn took his son was none of her concern.

"Not at all." Without taking his eyes off the road, Winn grasped her hand in his and gave it a squeeze. "You needn't be, either. I won't let anyone hurt him."

The words, said with such authority and certainty, had the ball of worry in Hailey's stomach dissolving.

"I'd like you to come with us tomorrow."

"Me?" Her voice rose and cracked. Spend her Sunday with a man who scared her spitless? *No, thanks.*

"The way I see it, the three of us are a team." Winn flashed a persuasive smile. "It's best for all members of a team to show solidarity when facing a potentially difficult situation."

"I don't know…" Hailey chewed on her bottom lip. She could only imagine what Jim might think—and say—if she showed up with Winn and Cam.

Because she was Tripp's sister, Jim *might* be nice to her. But the man was unpredictable and volatile.

As if he could read her thoughts, Winn's fingers tightened around hers. "What I said applies to you, too. I won't let him say or do anything to hurt you."

What about you? Hailey thought, looking at Winn's strong face that had become so familiar, so dear. *Who will protect you?*

She would. She would protect him.

"I'd love to go with you."

At Winn's quick smile, she chuckled.

"Okay, so maybe *love* is too strong a word. I—"

"My—my mommy loved me."

The small voice from the backseat had Hailey freezing.

"I know she did, buddy," Winn said with an easy manner that Hailey couldn't help admiring.

"Then why did she leave me?"

The question had been asked before and would no doubt be asked many times in the future, a plaintive cry of a little boy trying to make sense of all the changes in his world.

"She didn't want to leave you," Winn said with such surety any doubter would have been convinced. "Your mother never would have left you if she'd had a choice. But I'm here for you, son. I'm not going anywhere."

Silence filled the backseat for several heartbeats.

"Okay," Cam said finally.

Winn meant what he'd said. He would be there for his son. In time, Cam would see that while he might no longer have his mother, he could count on his dad.

The party was in full swing when they arrived. Cars lined both sides of the road as well as the circular driveway leading to the large two-story home. Winn finally found a spot on the road in front of a minivan.

"Just think, one day you'll be driving one of those beauties," Hailey told him.

Winn blanched.

"Don't worry." Hailey patted his arm. "From what I've heard, the decline happens in stages. You barely notice."

Though the sun still shone brightly, hurricane lanterns lined the walkway to the house, ready to be lit when the sun finally set.

Sunflowers with faces as big as dinner plates flanked the front door. Travis welcomed them, thumping Winn's back and kissing Hailey's cheek.

Dressed as Travis was in ultracasual jeans, a plaid shirt and sneakers, Hailey doubted anyone who didn't know Travis would peg him as one of the top ob-gyn physicians in Jackson Hole.

Travis took her hands and stepped back. "You're looking all grown-up and beautiful tonight."

Hailey felt a rush of pleasure. "I always said you were my favorite of Tripp's friends."

The father of five grinned, then turned to Winn.

"You better treat her right, Ferris. Hailey is like a little sister to me."

"I'd have thought you had enough sisters," Winn retorted, but there was no rancor in his tone.

"You can never have too many," Travis said diplomatically.

"Stop with the little-sister stuff." His wife appeared, looking cute as a button in a blue knit top and a flirty skirt dotted with tiny flowers. "Trust me, honey. Once a woman reaches a certain age, she doesn't want to be anyone's *little* sister. Am I correct, Hailey?"

Hailey knew that for a lot of years Mary Karen—known affectionately as MK—had been referred to as David Wahl's little sister.

"It's true, Travis," Hailey solemnly agreed.

Travis expelled a melodramatic sigh. "Once again I stand corrected." He cast his wife a glance, but even his downturned lips couldn't hide the twinkle in his eyes. "Why can't you be like the nurses at the hospital? They would never think to correct me."

"Even if that is true, which, by the way, I don't believe for a second, will the nurses at the hospital—?" His wife rose on tiptoe to whisper in his ear.

Travis's blue eyes widened then darkened. "Now?"

MK's eyes danced. "Soon."

The hostess shifted her gaze to the small boy standing silently at his dad's side. Dressed in jeans and a brightly striped tee, Cam shifted from one foot to the other, his eyes big as quarters, taking in the scene.

"Logan has been asking about you, Cam." Mary Karen's tone turned motherly. "He can't wait to play. Charlie just arrived."

She held out her hand. "I'll take you to the playroom."

To Hailey's surprise Cam hesitated and reached for *her* hand.

"If you decide you want to see your dad or Hailey at any time, we'll get them for you." MK spoke directly to the little boy, her voice soft and even. "In a little bit, we'll all get together for some fun activities in the backyard."

"W-what k-kind of a-a-activities?" Cam stammered.

"Croquet. Horseshoes. Badminton. Among other games."

A frown worried the boy's brow. "I—I don't know th-those g-games."

"They're fun," Winn told his son. "I'll teach you when it's time."

Mary Karen waited a moment then asked again. "Do you want me to take you to the boys now? Last I saw, they were playing with the train."

Hesitantly Cam released her hand. Hailey gave him a reassuring smile.

"I want to see the train," Hailey heard Cam say to Mary Karen as she led him toward the stairs going down to the playroom.

Hailey and Winn visited with Travis for only a minute before their host left to answer the door. Although a fair amount of people were gathered inside, she and Winn followed the laughter coming from the backyard.

They stepped outside into a cacophony of noise and color. There were several metal washtubs filled with ice and bottles of soda and beer. A mason-jar-inspired drink dispenser filled to the brim with lemonade held chunks of lemon as big as a man's thumb.

Scattered tables were covered with brightly patterned cloths featuring various summer flowers. Centerpieces composed of glass teapots held not only ice and tea but also edible flowers. Bunting strung above the tables, held up by baker's twine, added vintage charm.

Hailey widened her eyes at the sprigs of berries and leaves interspersed between the bunting. She felt a surge of excitement. While no one was currently kissing under the mistletoe, she knew it was only a matter of time before someone took advantage of the situation.

Would it be her and Winn who kicked off that tradition? Or was it a promise of a kiss that Mary Karen had whispered into her husband's ear only minutes earlier?

Hailey spotted Tripp and Anna chatting with Meg and Cole. When her sister-in-law saw her, a smile lit her pretty features. It froze on her lips when Anna noticed who was with her.

"Chickadee," a booming voice called out behind her. "You've finally arrived. Now this party can get started."

Hailey turned to see Cassidy hustling toward them in three-inch orange heels. Atomic-yellow leggings looked painted on and the black tunic top boasted a huge orange-and-yellow sunflower. The hairstylist had continued the look with tiny flowers woven through her blond curls.

"You look fab, Cass."

Cassidy held her at arm's length and studied her from head to toe. "Those shoes are totally mag. And your hair is incredible. The clothes are…nice…albeit a trifle on the boring side."

Beside her, Winn stifled a laugh.

Hailey lifted a brow. "Albeit?"

"Just trying to punch up the vocab. Conversations can be so boring." Cassidy shifted her gaze to Winn. "I don't believe I've ever seen you so delectably casual, Ferris."

Winn jerked a head in Hailey's direction. "Her influence."

Cassidy brought an orange-and-purple-tipped finger to her lips then nodded. "Yes, I see it now."

The stylist shifted her gaze to Hailey and she felt herself begin to blush. Something about Cassidy's scrutiny made her feel like a wayward child caught with her hand in the cookie jar.

Cassidy wrapped her fingers around Winn's muscular biceps and batted her lashes. "I do so love a strong, virile man."

"Keep your hands to yourself, Cass," Hailey warned.

Winn grinned. But the smile vanished when Cassidy pinned him with those bright blue eyes.

"I sense something sizzling between you and my girl," Cassidy said in a tone that would make a fortune-teller proud.

"Cass," Hailey hissed as several people standing nearby turned.

"What red-blooded man wouldn't be attracted to Hailey?" Winn's tone was light. "She's intelligent and beautiful. That's a potent combination."

Cassidy's blue eyes turned cool. "Are you going to break her heart like that scumbag Gratzke?"

"Josh didn't break my heart, Cass," Hailey huffed. But neither of them appeared to be listening to her.

"I don't intend to, no."

"Okay, then." Like a queen bestowing absolution on her subjects, Cassidy fluttered her hand in the warm summer air. "Go forth and multiply."

"What?" Hailey squeaked.

"I meant, go forth and have fun," Cassidy amended. "I'm going to mingle and see—"

The hairstylist stopped midsentence, her shocked gaze focused in the distance.

Hailey tracked the direction. Dr. Tim Duggan stood laughing with Travis. A brown-haired woman dressed conservatively in khakis and a mint-green shirt stood beside Tim with her arm looped through his.

"Who's the woman with Tim?" Winn asked. "I don't recall seeing her before."

"Jayne Connors," Hailey said.

Cassidy squinted behind her yellow-and-black cat's-eye glasses. "Plain Jayne? I don't think so."

"It is," Hailey insisted. "I ran into her at the grocery store a month or so ago."

Winn's eyebrow arched. "Plain Jayne?"

"Her nickname in high school." Cassidy snapped her chewing gum. "Isn't she a librarian or something?"

"I'm not sure about her occupation. We only spoke for a few minutes in the produce aisle." Hailey studied the couple. They looked good together. "My mother says her mom and Tim's mother are thrilled they've started seeing each other."

"Why?" Cassidy asked bluntly, her expression inscrutable.

"The two mothers are BFFs. They've wanted Jayne and Tim to get together since they were babies."

"Just because he's hanging with her at some stupid party doesn't mean anything," Cassidy insisted.

Hailey couldn't figure out why Cassidy even cared. "I guess—"

"As fascinating as this conversation has become," Winn interrupted, "David Wahl just stepped outside. He's head of the zoning committee. I want to catch him before the party takes off."

"It's always business with you, Ferris," Cassidy said mildly.

"Business and sex," Winn said sardonically. "What else is there?"

Cassidy lifted her hands, let them drop. "Truer words."

Winn squeezed Hailey's shoulder, met her gaze. "I'll catch up with you in a few minutes."

He sauntered off and Cassidy gave a low whistle.

"Mr. Dark and De-Lish." Cassidy licked her lips. "What's he like in the sack?"

"Why are you asking me?"

Cassidy's gaze narrowed. "You really expect me to believe you and he haven't done the deed?"

"The deed is still undone," Hailey confirmed. She saw no need to mention they'd rounded second base on the sofa the other night.

"What the hell are you waiting for? The Second Coming?"

"Let's just say the opportunity hasn't presented itself... yet." Thinking of her earlier premonition, Hailey shivered in anticipation.

"Don't wait too long." Cassidy's gaze shifted briefly back to Tim and Jayne. "Otherwise, some early bird may end up getting your worm."

Chapter Twelve

"The night is still young." Winn fingered the sprig of berries and leaves in his pocket. "Plenty of time for kissing once we get home."

Home with Hailey.

Why did it sound so right?

Before opening the car door, Winn linked his fingers with hers. He brought her hand to his mouth and placed a kiss in the palm.

"Since Cam is having a sleepover, perhaps you'd be interested in one as well." He kept his voice casual and offhand. "My bed. Pajamas optional."

"I don't wear pajamas." The words came out in a throaty purr.

Winn felt a tightening in his groin. "Is that so?"

She flashed an impish smile. "Not really. I just always wanted to say it."

Winn reached for the door handle then stopped. She

hadn't said yes. Without warning, he yanked her to him and kissed her until she moaned and went limp against him.

"Say you'll stay with me tonight," he urged, nuzzling her neck.

"Yes," she said breathlessly.

But when he tried to kiss her again, Hailey placed a palm against his chest and pushed him back.

"No more kisses until we get home," she said in a prim schoolmarm-type voice that turned him inside out. "Or I may be tempted to pull you to the ground and have my way with you right here."

Winn glanced down at the gravel road and winced. Making love to Hailey on the side of a road would be a memorable event but for all the wrong reasons. He could wait the twenty minutes until they got home.

Then he'd make it a night to remember…for both of them.

Hailey kept the conversation light all the way home. By the time Winn pulled into the garage, her heart felt as if it had been invaded by jumping beans.

At the top of the stairs, she paused to twine her arms around his neck. The last thing she wanted to do was leave him now, but it couldn't be helped. She ran her fingers through his thick, silky hair. "Give me ten minutes. I have to take Bandit out and then make sure he has food and water."

Winn's gaze searched hers before he gave her a hard kiss that curled her toes. "I'll be waiting."

Once inside her apartment, Hailey hooked Bandit to the leash with trembling hands. Thinking of Winn and his hot, persuasive lips had her quickening her steps. She hurried Bandit to the patch of grass at the front of the building.

As the dog sniffed and moseyed from one bush to another, Hailey tried to curb her impatience. Now that the "perfect" time had arrived she didn't want to waste a second.

She hadn't been kidding when she'd told Winn she was ready to pull him to the ground. His kisses had ignited a fierce yearning. But the yearning went beyond sexual need. The connection between her and Winn was one she'd never experienced with any other man.

This connection mattered. The fact that it did scared her to death. The feelings she'd had for Josh had been a pale imitation of what she felt for Winn.

Tonight had been their first night out together as a couple. Now she was going to sleep with him. Was she being foolish? Impulsive?

Probably.

Despite her growing feelings for Winn, she was entering into this liaison with eyes wide open.

No promises of forever.

No thoughts of a white picket fence and 2.5 kids.

Only one thing was on this evening's agenda. Hailey's breasts began to tingle and an ache formed low in her belly.

When Bandit finally took care of business and headed up the steps, she was at his heels. In minutes, he was fed and watered and she was at Winn's door.

It opened immediately after her light rap, as if he'd been standing on the other side waiting. His feet were bare but otherwise he looked the same. The same, yet somehow different. The hard shell he presented to the world was gone, replaced by a more vulnerable man.

"May I get you a glass of wine?" He gestured vaguely in the direction of the kitchen, his gaze never leaving her face. "Or a cup of coffee?"

She looped her arms around his neck, planting a kiss at the base of his throat, his skin salty beneath her lips. "I want you."

Something flickered in the backs of his eyes. "You're everything I want, Hailey."

The intensity of his declaration disturbed her. Tonight was supposed to be a romp, light and fun.

"Why are we standing here talking?" Hailey cocked her head. "Shouldn't we be getting naked?"

He grinned, the lines of his face easing, making him look more carefree. "I think you've been hanging around Cassidy Kaye just a little too long."

"Just keeping it real." Despite the bold words, Hailey found herself blushing.

"I like your reality." Winn brushed a strand of hair back from her face with a gentle hand.

Hailey was startled when Winn grabbed her hand. Tugging her to the sofa, he sat and pulled her down beside him.

"You want to…talk?" Hailey couldn't keep the disappointment from her voice.

A smile tugged at the corners of his lips as he shook his head and pointed to the ceiling.

She tilted her head back. Directly over their heads, a tiny sprig of mistletoe hung from the ceiling fan. Hailey laughed aloud. "Where did you get that?"

"Swiped it from the party." His tone was smug and unrepentant.

"I love bad boys." Hailey gazed at him through lowered lashes. "It'd be almost criminal to go to all that trouble and not make use of it."

"My thoughts exactly." He'd barely finished speaking, when his lips closed over hers.

He kissed her with a slow thoroughness that left her weak, trembling and longing for more. When his tongue swept across her lips, she eagerly opened her mouth to him.

Skilled hands skimmed up her sides, one thumb brushed against the tip of her nipple as his mouth melded with hers.

Hailey had done her share of kissing in her twenty-seven years, starting when she was fourteen at a freshman dance. But never had she been kissed like this. Slow kisses that made her feel drunk with need. Deep kisses that made her body ache with fiery passion.

She pressed against him, wanting to get closer. His

strong, clever hands answered her unspoken plea, sliding under her shirt to scorch her already burning flesh.

After he removed her shirt, the feel of his hands on her belly made her want to squirm. Up or down. She needed him to move those hands up or down. As if he'd heard her plea, his nimble fingers rose and unclasped her bra.

"You're beautiful." He lowered his head, his breath warm against her bare flesh.

His tongue circled the nipple, licking the sensitive skin until she felt she'd go mad if he didn't take the aching bud into his mouth. She arched back.

"Please," she whimpered.

His mouth closed over the peak, drawing it fully into his mouth. He suckled gently, then harder.

Tension filled her body. His fingers curled around the waistband of her pants and she eagerly lifted her hips so he could slip them off. The lacy thong she wore underneath brought a flash of heat to his eyes and a smile to his lips.

His hand slipped beneath the scrap of fabric, through the curls and between her legs. She parted for him, catching her breath as he rubbed against her slick center.

Hailey's need for him was so strong that all it took was for him to slide one finger inside for the orgasm to hit.

She pushed against his hand and sobbed as his tongue plunged into her mouth.

He held her while the climax rippled through her, murmuring endearments. Then she felt herself being carried to the bedroom. The navy sheets had been pulled back. He deposited her on the bed and his clothes joined her thong on the floor.

Then he was kissing her all over. The raw need, her desire for him, returned full force.

"Tell me what you like," she whispered, reaching for him.

"Tonight is about you," he murmured. "Our first night, but it won't be our last."

The kisses began again and the touching, oh, the wonderful feel of his hands on her skin...

Scattering kisses down her neck and lower, he created a trail of heat. Hailey squirmed as the need inside her began to build once again.

His lips reached her belly and when he edged her knees apart, she realized what he meant to do. She pressed her legs together—or tried to—but his hands kept them spread and his mouth was suddenly where no mouth had gone before.

The sight of his dark head between her legs was incredibly erotic. She squirmed, but not to get away. The sensation of his hot breath against her core, the tongue dipping and swirling, had her arching back.

"I can't take this," she panted, digging her heels into the mattress and clutching the sheets with her hands. "I need you inside me."

She felt him hesitate, heard the tear of a foil packet, then he was over her and with one hard plunge, inside her.

He was thick and hard and filled her completely. She wrapped her legs around him, taking in the whole length of him. Then they began to move in a rhythm as old as Time.

Desire and pleasure and raw need were so strong, Hailey felt as if she might explode.

Winn was patient, pushing her steadily toward that crest with long, deep kisses and clever hands that caressed.

She felt the orgasm building, tried to slow it down, wanting to savor the sensations a little while longer.

In and out. In and out.

She dropped her hands to his hips and pulled him closer. Deeper. The tension began to build again.

Her breath now coming in ragged puffs, Hailey strained toward him. Reaching, needing, wanting.

In and out. In and out. Until she felt her grip slip and she came apart in his arms, crying out as waves of pleasure engulfed her.

He kept up the rhythm until every last ounce of pleasure had been wrung from her body, then gave one final thrust and found his own release, calling out her name.

They lay there, ragged breaths mingling. She felt the rapid thump of his heart against hers.

"Wow," Hailey finally managed to mumble. "If I'd known it'd be like this between us, I'd have jumped you the first night."

Winn's lips lifted in an easy, satisfied smile. "Ditto."

Hailey giggled. The movement made her aware he was still inside her. She supposed she could have asked him to move, but she didn't. She liked things just the way they were for the moment.

"I think I'm crushing you."

He shifted, but she wrapped her arms around his neck. "Not yet."

Something in her soft tone must have gotten through, because he stilled. Or perhaps it was the feel of her fingers combing through his hair.

"You always look so put together." She smiled up at him. "I like seeing you this way."

"Naked?"

"Disheveled. But naked is nice, too." Her expression sobered. "It's like I'm seeing a part of you that's just for me."

"Hailey. I—"

She placed her mouth to his lips in a gentle kiss before he could say more. "Enjoy the moment."

"I think you'll enjoy it more if you didn't have a hundred and eighty pounds pressing you into the mattress."

Ignoring her protests, he rolled off her. She thought he meant to get up, maybe send her on her way. Instead, he tugged her to him.

"There," he said, warm and relaxed next to her. "This is better."

"This *is* nice." Her fingers toyed with the light dusting of hair on his chest. For a business executive who spent much of his day on the phone or in meetings, he was incredibly fit.

She'd thought things might be awkward between them… after…but he'd made everything so easy and right by pulling her close. When he held her like this, she felt as if she was exactly where she was meant to be.

But while she was sure there would be another night, Hailey knew there was no guarantee. She wouldn't waste this opportunity.

Without warning, she flipped over on top of him, bracketing her arms on either side of his muscular torso. "Now that I have you just where I want you, I have some inventive ideas of what we could do next."

"Inventive?" A devilish gleam filled his eyes as he rolled the word around on his tongue. "I have several crazy ideas of my own."

"Do we have to pick?" Hailey leaned down and flicked her tongue against the tip of his nipple. "Can't we be both inventive and a little crazy?"

She took his moan of pleasure to be an affirmative. As her hand lowered to stroke the silky length of him, the phone on the nightstand buzzed.

Hailey's hand paused midstroke. She glanced at the bedside clock. "Who'd be calling you at 3:00 a.m.?"

Winn reached out and grabbed the phone. His gaze swept the readout. "This is Winn. What's up, Meg?"

While he talked, Hailey rolled to the side. Immediately he hopped out of bed and began dressing with one hand.

Hailey slipped away to get her clothes. When she returned fully dressed, Winn was ready to leave.

"What happened?"

"Apparently, Cam woke up sobbing." Winn raked a hand through his already mussed hair. "Meg spent the last half hour trying to calm him."

"I'll come with you."

He hesitated, then gathered her close against him in a brief embrace. "Thank you."

"We can take Bandit," Hailey said. "The dog can sit next to him on the car ride home. You know what a comfort Bandit can be to him."

To Winn's credit, he didn't even blanch at the suggestion of allowing the dog on his Mercedes's cream-colored seats.

But, conscious of the buttery leather, Hailey grabbed a cotton throw for the dog to sit on.

There wasn't much conversation during the twenty-minute drive to the Lassiter home.

"As the oldest girl in a family of eight, if anyone can give Cam motherly comfort, it's Meg," Hailey assured him, feeling the need to fill the void of worried silence.

"I knew she and Travis came from a large family." Winn's eyes remained firmly fixed on the dark and winding mountain road. "I didn't realize there were that many kids. Wow."

"Do you want children?"

"That's an odd question." He cast a quick sideways glance. "Considering we're on the way to pick up my eight-year-old son."

"Not so odd." Hailey kept her voice calm. "You said Vanessa getting pregnant was a surprise. I just wondered if you want more children in the future."

He slowed to turn onto a side road. "Sure," he said. "I like kids. What about you?"

Hailey kept her voice equally offhand. "Maybe two or three. Someday."

"Good numbers." Winn turned into the driveway leading to the large mountain home.

"Better than seven or eight," Hailey quipped, and he chuckled.

But his expression was grim as they reached the porch. Cole must have been waiting for them, because the door opened before they had a chance to knock. His eyes widened slightly when he saw Hailey.

"We hated to call—"

"How's he doing?" Winn interrupted, his eyes dark with concern.

"He quit crying about five minutes ago." Cole ushered them into an impressive foyer that went up at least twelve feet.

"Meg brought him down to the living room." Cole's gray eyes were filled with sympathy. "He was very upset."

"I shouldn't have let him spend the night." Winn's expression turned tortured. "It was too soon."

"It's okay," Hailey crooned, and gave his hand a supportive squeeze.

"Don't beat yourself up about it. Charlie had lots of highs and lows when he first came to live with me and Meg. He'd seem fine, then he'd cry for his mother. Seeing Dr. Peter Allman helped. I hear a child psychologist recently joined Pete's practice."

"I'll check that out," Winn murmured as his steps quickened.

They'd reached the doorway to the living room when Hailey touched Winn's arm. "I can hang back here and wait if you think that'd be better."

Surprise flickered across his face. He took her hand. "No. I'm sure he'll want to see you."

Cole said nothing, though Hailey knew those assessing gray eyes missed nothing.

Cam sat on the sofa next to Meg, both still in their nightclothes. Meg had on a silky yellow robe cinched around her waist, while Cam wore a pair of Spider-Man pj's he must have borrowed from Charlie. The boy's face was tear-streaked and he glanced down when he saw Winn.

"Hey, sport." Winn stepped forward and took a seat beside him. "I hear you've had a rough night."

"I had a d-dream. I—I saw Mommy." The boy looked up

at Winn with reddened eyes and a lip that trembled. "But when I w-woke up she wasn't there."

Two plump tears spilled down his cheeks.

Winn seemed at a loss for words.

Hailey had a feeling he'd be making an appointment with the psychologist first thing on Monday. "Hailey and I came to take you home."

"Hailey?" Cam looked up, appearing to notice her for the first time.

"Hi, sweetie," she said softly. "Bandit insisted on coming, too. He's out in the car waiting for you."

The child's eyes brightened. He turned to Meg. "B-Bandit is a dog. H-he's Hailey's dog, b-but he likes me, too."

"He loves to play fetch," Hailey told Meg. "Perhaps Charlie can come over sometime this week and the boys can give Bandit some exercise."

"Would you like that, Cam?" Meg asked.

Cam hesitated. "Charlie might n-not want to come. Because I—I was a big baby."

"Charlie used to have nightmares, too," Meg said gently.

A young child's cry broke the momentary silence.

"Looks like Evie is up." Cole gave his wife's shoulder a squeeze. "I'll take care of her. You stay—"

"Tend to your daughter. We're heading out, anyway." Winn rose and extended a hand to Cole. "Thanks for everything."

Their palms connected in a brief shake. Cole's eyes met Winn's. "Like my wife said, we've been down this road. If you ever want to talk—"

The baby's cry rent the air once again and, after giving Cam a quick hug, Meg hurried from the room.

For the first time since they'd arrived, Cole's gaze lingered on Hailey. "Seeing you tonight was an unexpected pleasure."

There was something in those cool gray eyes that made

Hailey wonder if her name—and late-night visit—might come up in a future conversation with her brother.

She lifted her chin and smiled at Cole, reminding herself only one thing mattered right now...the child with the tear-streaked face and haunted eyes sitting on the sofa.

Chapter Thirteen

In a matter of minutes, Hailey, Winn and Cam were in the car and headed down the mountain. Cam sat in the backseat, Bandit sprawled protectively across his lap.

He was so small to be dealing with so much. But Cam was resilient, she reminded herself. For a second she'd wondered if she should have remained at home, but seeing Cam's response to her and Bandit had told her coming with Winn had been the right move.

They hadn't even turned onto the main highway into Jackson and the boy was already asleep. "Looks like he's down for the count."

Winn's finger visibly tightened on the steering wheel. "He's too young to have to deal with all this."

"Sometimes life doesn't give us a choice."

Other than the glow from the state-of-the-art instrument panel, darkness permeated the silent Mercedes. While it might be the perfect place for confidences, it wasn't a perfect time. Hailey wasn't in the mood to talk about herself or her relationship with Winn.

What they'd shared earlier had shaken her to the core. Right now she didn't want to think what the feelings he'd stirred in her might mean, much less chat about them.

Besides, knowing how worried he must be about Cam, Winn needed a distraction, not more drama.

"Have you always liked to golf?" she asked, settling on a topic guaranteed to get good conversational mileage.

He cast a quizzical glance in her direction. "Where did that come from?"

"We're getting to know each other." Hailey kept her tone light. "Talking about things that are important is essential to a budding friendship."

"After what happened earlier, I believe it's safe to say we're well past the budding stage."

"Point taken." Hailey snorted back a laugh. "But I'd still like you to answer my question."

"I loved the game from my first day on the links." Winn's shoulders, which had been military straight, relaxed. "Though how much of that enjoyment was simply spending time with my granddad and away from my father, I couldn't say."

"Your father didn't golf with you?"

"My dad only plays with men at his level." Amusement filled Winn's eyes. "Unless he thinks it might further a business deal."

"Why doesn't that surprise me?" Hailey drawled, then clapped a hand over her mouth. Regardless of her feelings for Jim, the man *was* Winn's father.

Winn didn't appear to notice her faux pas. Or if he did, he didn't take offense.

"My grandfather believed golf was more than a game," Winn said, almost to himself, "and that playing it would teach me valuable life lessons."

Hailey visualized a little white ball—or her favorite pink one—sailing down a fairway. Other than her need to work on her swing, she tried to think what her golfing experience had taught her.

"I know you're supposed to keep your mouth shut while someone is teeing off…" Hailey brought a finger to her lips, thinking hard. "I suppose a takeaway could be we need to respect a person's right to have their time in the spotlight."

Winn's smile flashed. "Excellent analogy."

She laughed. "I'm glad you like it because it's all I've got." She pointed to Winn. "Back to you, Ferris."

He stopped the car at a light and shifted in his seat to face her. Winn's gaze lingered on her face with such intensity that Hailey felt heat creeping up her neck.

"The game helps a person develop a sense of personal responsibility," Winn responded as the light changed and he shifted his gaze to the road ahead. "You can't blame a wrong choice of driver on anyone other than yourself."

"What about a caddy?" Not that she'd ever had anyone carry *her* clubs and make suggestions, but she'd certainly watched her share of tournaments on the Golf Channel.

"The caddy suggests," he pointed out. "Ultimately the choice is yours."

Hailey nodded.

"Granddad emphasized the game is about managing emotions. That one struck home." Winn spoke quietly, but she sensed intense emotion simmering just beneath his tightly held composure. "You and I both know things don't always go our way. We can triple bogey in life as easily as we can on the course. What's essential is keeping perspective and focusing on the next shot."

"Your grandfather sounds like a wise man." Impulsively Hailey leaned over and kissed Winn's cheek. "Like grandfather like grandson."

A quick smile was his only response.

She may have started the conversation as a pleasant diversion but found herself wanting to know more.

"Is that why you got involved with a company that develops courses? Because you love the game so much?" Hailey pressed.

"I golfed in college, at one time thought about turning pro. Then I did an internship at a company started by Arnold Palmer. It specialized in golf-course design. I'd found my niche."

"How'd you end up at GPG?" From what Tripp had told her, the company was more of an investment firm.

"Once I finished my master's in landscape architecture, I did an apprenticeship at GPG."

"Do you plan to stay with them?" From the time in his home, Hailey had discovered Winn was a busy man,. His job didn't leave him much free time.

"If the development here falls through, I might not have a choice," Winn said in a matter-of-fact tone. "They'll probably give me the boot."

Shocked, Hailey straightened in her seat. Anger rippled through her veins. "Surely they realize you don't have control over the approval process."

"Doesn't matter. If the project is turned down, it'll be on me." His expression turned contemplative. "The sad thing is, the design is top-notch. I incorporated all the principles of a good ecosystem."

Puzzled, Hailey cocked her head. "I'm not sure what that means."

"Providing wildlife habitat, protecting topsoil from wind and water erosion, things like that."

"Does my brother know all this?"

"He should. It's in the report." Winn pulled the car to a stop and shut off the ignition.

Hailey looked around, startled to realize they were home. She fought a surge of disappointment. She wasn't ready for the conversation to end. She and Winn may have been physically intimate, but she'd barely scratched the surface of who he was as a person. She was eager to hear his

views on any number of issues. Hailey especially wanted
to learn more about his design work.

"Where are we?" Cam rubbed sleep-filled eyes and fumbled with his seat belt.

"We're home." Winn twisted in his seat, his gaze searching his son's face as if looking for signs of any of his earlier distress.

Cam stroked the dog's back. "Can Bandit spend the
night? Just this once? Please?"

Hailey pushed open the car and stepped out. Following
her lead, Cam got out, too. As soon as the door opened,
Bandit launched himself from the boy's lap and sprinted
to a nearby tree.

"Please, Daddy." Looking small and defenseless in his
Spider-Man pj's, Cam fixed his pleading gaze on his dad.

"I need to speak with Hailey before I make that decision." Winn's tone was firm, brooking no argument. "While
she and I discuss the matter, I'd like you to stand right there
and keep your eyes on Bandit."

When Cam eagerly nodded and turned to watch the dog,
Winn gently grasped Hailey's arm and pulled her out of
the child's earshot.

"It's okay with me if he stays—"

Winn's mouth closing over hers stopped the words. His
kiss was warm and persuasive, leaving her lips tingling
when he pulled back.

"Forget the dog," he said in a husky voice that had her
insides scrambling. "Will *you* stay?"

She glanced in Cam's direction. His eyes were still
firmly focused on the dog. Hailey lowered her voice.
"We've discussed this before. Not while Cam is there."

Winn slid a hand up her arm. "Is there anything I can
say—or do—to change your mind?"

Hailey shook her head. Still, she couldn't resist wrapping
her arms around Winn one more time. She held him close.

But before she could give in to temptation, she stepped back and called out to Cam. "Take good care of my Bandito."

Cam whirled. "He can stay with me?"

"All night." Winn glanced at his wrist. "That is, what's left of it."

"Yippee." Cam bent over and gave Bandit a fierce hug. "C'mon, boy."

Hailey and Winn followed Cam as he and the dog bounded up the stairs.

"If you change your mind, you have the key." Winn's tone was low, the words for her ears only.

"If you recall, you made it clear that was for emergency use only."

His gaze met hers. "I'm sending out an official SOS."

She smiled. Then resolutely, and with more than a little regret, Hailey turned in the direction of her condo and her own bed.

When her alarm went off the next morning, Hailey was tempted to simply roll over. Instead, she hopped out of bed and hit the shower. Securing her hair into a low twist, she slipped on the blue eyelet dress she'd gotten on sale last week. Then she grabbed her heeled sandals and was out the door in ten minutes.

She found a parking space a block from the café. As she clicked her car doors locked and hurried down the sidewalk, she wondered once again why she'd agreed to meet Anna and Tripp for breakfast.

Most of the group that met every week for breakfast attended church first. While their children were in Sunday school, couples hurried to the café for food and conversation with friends. Her brother and Anna were regulars, but the composition of the rest of those around the table was fluid and varied from week to week.

Hailey never felt as if she fully fit into the tight-knit group made up of young movers and shakers in the Jackson Hole community. She liked everyone a lot. It was just she had little in common with couples who had children and more settled lives. It was always nice to see Tripp and Anna, though she usually saw them at her parents' home every Sunday evening.

Tonight she'd spend with Winn and Cam at his father's ranch. Just the thought of Jim's sarcastic nature brought a sick feeling to the pit of her stomach. She wasn't concerned for herself but for Cam. Hailey determinedly pushed aside her trepidation. Winn would keep his dad on a short leash. Not an easy task, but if anyone was up to the challenge, it would be Winn.

Winn.

The lights had been dark in his condo this morning. Instead of knocking on his door to let him know her plans, she'd texted him. After such a late night, he and Cam deserved the extra rest. Still, she couldn't help thinking if she'd accepted his offer last night, she'd be snuggled up against his warm body right now.

Hailey expelled a resigned sigh. Sometimes doing the right thing sucked.

She entered the Coffee Pot, a popular café in downtown Jackson, and immediately began threading her way through the tables filled with chattering tourists and year-round residents, dressed in their Sunday best. Situated at the back of the dining room, so close to the kitchen you could hear bacon popping, a large rectangular table was reserved for the group every Sunday.

The waitress, an older woman with frizzy gray hair and bright orange lipstick, was well aware most at the table had only an hour to eat. She made it her mission to get them out in time to pick up their kids, knowing a generous tip would be her reward.

As Hailey drew close, she noticed there were still several empty seats at the table. Though her sister-in-law's back was to her, the lush chestnut hair made her easy to identify. "I'm sorry I'm late—"

A man stood and she skidded to a stop, her heart leaping with surprised pleasure.

Winn was pulling back the empty chair between him and Anna. "Good morning."

Hailey gaped. "Wh-what are you doing here?"

"Getting ready to order." Winn shot her a smile that made her heart stammer as much as her voice. "And, in case you're wondering, Cam is at Sunday school and Bandit is sleeping...on the sofa."

Hailey chuckled at his pained expression and dropped into the chair. She was conscious that Meg and Cole were staring with puzzled expressions.

Of all the people Hailey had thought might be here, it wasn't them. For chrissakes, they had two kids to get ready and had been up past 3:00 a.m.

"Winn was telling us that Cam slept well after he picked him up." Meg offered Hailey a reassuring smile.

While there was no guarantee that Cole wouldn't mention her late-night visit, the careful way Meg worded her comment didn't throw up any red flags.

"I'm happy you made it this morning," Kate Dennes said to Hailey. A dark-haired woman with green eyes, the young pediatrician was one of those women who always looked stylish and perfectly put together. This morning she wore a dress with bright yellow flowers cinched tight at the waist. "It seems like forever since we've had a chance to talk."

Her husband, Joel, a local contractor, paused with his coffee cup halfway to his lips, a puzzled look on his handsome face. "Didn't we just see her and Winn last night?"

Her and Winn.

Hailey wondered if she was the only one who'd caught the way Joel had lumped the two of them together, as if they were a couple.

"*Saw* her," Kate clarified to her husband. "We never got a chance to talk and catch up."

"Of course," Joel said as if that explained everything. He shifted his attention to attorney Nick Delacourt, who sat to his right.

"How's the job going?" Kate asked.

"Which one?" Hailey accepted a cup of coffee from the waitress, acutely conscious of Winn beside her.

Obviously startled, Kate lifted a perfectly tweezed brow. "How many do you have?"

"Three." The coffee was good, Hailey realized after taking a sip. Strong and black with just the kick she needed to get her system jump-started. "For now."

"Three?" Kate voice rose.

"It's not as bad as it sounds," Hailey said with a laugh. "I fill in at the hospital as needed. I help Cassidy Kaye with makeup for special events. And, as you know, I'm watching Cam for the summer."

"Such a sweet little boy." Kate's eyes softened and she shifted her gaze to Winn. "If you ever need a last-minute sitter, just give us a call. Chloe would love to mother Cam."

"I'll keep that in mind," Winn said, seeming touched by the offer. "Thank you."

"Winn told me he brought Cam in for his physical." Hailey glanced expectantly at Kate. "How'd it go?"

She'd meant to ask Winn last night about the visit, but then he kissed her and she kissed him back and they'd ended up in bed instead.

Kate smiled apologetically and gestured to Winn, making it clear that any information concerning that visit would have to come from him.

"It went well." The humorous glint in Winn's eyes told Hailey he, too, remembered what had forestalled the discussion. "I signed a release so Kate can get Cam's records from his family doctor in Georgia. She assured me he appears to be a healthy eight-year-old."

"He's a bright boy," Kate added.

"What about his stuttering?" Hailey directed the question to Kate.

Winn nodded in answer to Kate's raised brow.

"I need to see what his records show," Kate said. "Specifically when the stammering began and what steps have been taken to address the issue."

"Unless it began fairly recently," Hailey said.

"If that's the case, we'll know because nothing will be documented," Kate mused aloud.

Hailey turned to Winn. "You could always call his grandparents. That might be a faster way to get the information."

Though Winn stiffened, his voice was calm. "I could. But remember, they were upset with me for taking him."

"From their perspective, that's understandable." Hailey remembered the affection in Cam's voice when he spoke of Grandpa Larry and Grandma Jan. "Perhaps if you reach out—"

"Not a chance," Winn said flatly. "Not when they're talking about blocking my adoption."

"What?" The warmth that had enveloped Hailey when she'd first sat down disappeared in an arctic blast.

"It may be an idle threat," Winn said, "but it's something I intend to take seriously."

Across the table, Hailey saw Nick Delacourt's eyes sharpen.

"Threats like those should always be taken seriously." The attorney lifted his coffee cup and took a sip.

Winn's gaze met Nick's. "I'd like to schedule some time for us to talk this week."

Nick was a well-known family-law attorney with offices in Dallas and Jackson Hole. Several years ago, he'd briefly lost his memory in a skiing accident. His wife, Lexi—then a single mother—had been the social worker assigned to his case during that time.

Nick nodded. "I'll tell my assistant to expect your call."

Hailey had more questions about the threats Cam's grandparents had made and she wanted to know why Winn hadn't mentioned them to her before. But now wasn't the time for such a discussion.

The conversation around the table shifted to everyone's plans for the upcoming Fourth of July holiday. Hailey found it difficult to focus. Her mind kept skittering back to Cam's grandparents and what it would do to Winn if he lost his son again. And, what it would do to Cam.

Out of the corner of her eye, she watched a distinguished-looking man with salt-and-pepper hair approach her table and stop by her brother's chair. He didn't stay even long enough for introductions. Apparently he only wanted to commend Tripp on several of his community-improvement projects.

Once the man was out of earshot, Lexi exhaled a melo-dramatic sigh. "Another Tripp fan. How do you inspire such adoration?"

Looking slightly embarrassed, her brother only chuck-led.

"Tripp is a natural-born leader," Hailey told Lexi. "Even when we were kids, I can't remember a time when I wasn't trailing along in his shadow."

Winn twisted in a move so abrupt, she found herself shrinking back when he faced her.

"You—" he pointed at her chest "—don't trail in any-one's shadow. You make a difference in the lives of every-one you touch, just as much as he does."

Winn gestured with his head toward Tripp, who was watching the scene with intense interest.

"You don't have to defend me, Winn," Hailey said in a matter-of-fact tone. "There's nothing I do—"

"What about Cam?"

"What about him?"

"I've heard you working with him in the other room while I've been in my office."

"I'm sorry," she said, instantly contrite. "I tried to keep the noise down so we wouldn't disturb you."

Those hazel eyes fixed on hers and in that moment, everyone around them disappeared and there was just her and Winn.

"Listen." He took her shoulders in his hands, gave her a little shake. "You don't disturb me. You impress the heck out of me."

Hailey blinked. "What? How?"

"The speech games you play with my son, for starters. He doesn't realize they're therapy. He just thinks he's having fun."

Her lips quirked upward. "Education doesn't have to be boring."

"You give him your total attention, make him feel important, teach him techniques that help with his stammering." Winn's broad hand gently cupped her face. Apparently with no thought to anyone at the table, he pressed his lips against her, the kiss as gentle as softly falling rain. "You have a gift. Not just as a speech therapist but as a caring, giving woman. I'm certain he's not the only child or person whose life is better because of knowing you."

There was no subterfuge in his eyes. These were no empty compliments. He meant every word. Winn Ferris thought she was something special.

"Thank you," she murmured past the sudden lump in her throat. Then she said it again, more loudly this time in case he hadn't heard. "Thank you."

"It's true," Anna said softly, her hand reaching over to give Hailey's hand a squeeze. "Everything he said about you is true."

By the time the waitress arrived to take their order, both Hailey and Anna were blinking back tears. Thankfully, by the time all the food had been ordered and their coffee cups refilled, the talk had turned to baseball and the College World Series.

"Looks like UCLA will take it all this year," Winn commented just as his phone dinged. He glanced down, opened the text and silently read the message.

"Your mom is going to work with me on my knitting after supper," Anna said to Hailey as the men continued their CWS talk. "I thought it'd be fun if we could practice together."

"I'm afraid I won't be there," Hailey said with real regret. "Winn and I are going with Cam to his father's for dinner."

"Change in plans," Winn said, and she wondered at the irritation in his eyes. "I just got a text. My dad extended his stay in Philly. Hot business deal."

Was it wrong, Hailey wondered, to feel so relieved?

"So I'll see you tonight?" Anna asked eagerly.

Hailey turned to Winn. "Want to go to my parents' for dinner?"

"I appreciate the invitation." Winn pocketed his phone. "But Cam didn't get much sleep last night. I think we'll stay home, maybe get a pizza."

"Pot roast is much better for the kid than pizza," Tripp interjected. "And, if you come, it'll be a good chance for us to talk. I have some questions that were brought to me on the golf project."

Winn hesitated and glanced at Hailey.

"You know there's nothing better than my mom's pot roast," was all she said.

"Count us in," Winn said.

Hailey wanted him and Cam to come, truly she did. She only wished she knew if Winn had finally agreed because of her…or because of her brother.

Chapter Fourteen

"Are you certain your mother won't mind two more at the table tonight?" Winn asked as they strolled up the walk to the porch.

Cam had raced ahead but stopped at the door. While he waited for them to catch up, he put Bandit through his arsenal of tricks.

Hailey shifted her attention back to the man at her side. "My mother was delighted you were coming."

Delighted but *suspicious*. There was no need to mention that part of the conversation to Winn. He didn't need to know the concerns her mother had expressed over the time she was spending with Winn when she was "off duty."

Apparently, Anna had mentioned something about them being at the Coffee Pot this morning. Her mom had incorrectly assumed they'd arrived together.

"That's a relief," Winn said, and Hailey pulled her thoughts back to the present.

"It's always a plus when the host and hostess are genuinely happy to see you," he continued, shoving his hands into his pockets.

Hailey slipped her arm through his. "Trust me. Having you and Cam along makes everyone's evening more pleasurable."

Winn stopped at the bottom of the stairs and turned her to face him. His eyes met hers and the blood in her veins began to hum. He cupped her face with one hand and those beautiful hazel eyes grew dark.

He's going to kiss me. He's going to kiss me. The words repeated over and over like a mantra.

Her heart sped up, tripping over itself. She moistened her lips with the tip of her tongue, anticipating the feel of him, the sweet taste of him.

She lifted her face just as the front screen door banged open.

The sound was like a gunshot. Hailey jerked back so suddenly she stumbled. But Winn's hands remained on her shoulders, steadying her.

"If you two are finished gawking at each other," Frank called out as Cam and Bandit slipped past him into the house, "your mother could use some help in the kitchen."

Hailey saw the flash of resignation in Winn's eyes as he dropped his hands. But when he shifted his gaze to her father standing on the porch, his smile was warm and easy.

"Your daughter is so pretty, I have to gawk," Winn said, and Hailey felt the heat of a blush stain her cheeks. "By the way, I appreciate the dinner invitation."

Winn took Hailey's arm as they climbed the stairs, not seeming to notice the slight narrowing of her father's gaze.

Ever since they'd made love, there was a physical ease between her and Winn that hadn't existed before. Hailey reminded herself she wasn't sixteen anymore. Still, in her father's eyes, she'd always be his little girl. Woe to the man who hurt her.

Will you hurt me, Winn?

The second the thought surfaced, Hailey shoved it aside. They were friends. That's all.

"We're glad to have you." Her father clapped Winn on the back and ushered them inside. "But I'm warning you, after we eat, I need some muscle, so I'll be putting you to work."

A smile hovered at the corners of Winn's lips. "Just what kind of work do you have planned for me, Frank?"

Seeing Winn's dark tailored pants, Ralph Lauren shirt and Berluti loafers, Hailey could only hope that whatever her dad had in store for his guest didn't involve physical labor of the grimy sort.

His father's grin flashed and the wicked gleam in his eye told her he sensed her discomfort.

"Don't worry—" Frank waved a dismissive hand "—it doesn't involve cattle."

"I wasn't worried." A hint of coolness crept into Winn's tone. "Simply curious."

"*I'm* the one who's worried." Hailey pointed at her father. "I've seen some of your 'projects.'"

She paused, though there was much more she could have said, as sounds of frantic barking came from inside the house.

"Sounds like Bandit treed a squirrel in the kitchen," Frank said mildly.

Hailey cast a worried glance in her dad's direction as the dog continued to bark. "I hope you don't mind that we, I mean I, brought him."

"He's a good dog." Frank frowned as the noise escalated. "Even if he is kind of loud."

Cam came running down the hall, his eyes wide. "You gotta c-come. Bandit is going to kill it."

A shriek from the kitchen had both men running.

"What is it?" Hailey asked the boy, sprinting down the hall after the men.

"A snake," Cam said. "It's humongous."

* * *

"I can't believe there was a snake in the house." Anna gave a little shudder. She lifted a cup of steaming coffee to her lips but didn't drink. "I guess I should be happy Mindy Bigg's baby delayed his entrance into the world long enough to make us a few minutes late."

"Today, being a midwife was definitely a lucky thing." Hailey shivered. "I hate any kind of reptiles, too."

Hailey, Anna and her mother sat at the kitchen table enjoying their coffee while a full dishwasher hummed happily in the background.

By the time Tripp and Anna arrived, the men had removed the three-foot-long garter snake from the kitchen and taken it down to the creek to release it. Out of Cam's earshot, Frank laughingly reported the boy had begged Winn to let him keep it as a pet. His pleas had apparently fallen on deaf ears and the snake had slithered off into the brush.

The snake had turned the dinner conversation into story hour. Everyone at the table—other than Winn—had a crazy animal-encounter story to share. Even Cam. With exaggerated gestures, the boy told about a skink in the house that made his mother scream.

At everyone's baffled expressions, Winn explained that skink was another name for chameleon, and they were quite common in the south.

Winn asked questions and laughed at the outlandish and obviously embellished tales with an easy smile.

His background had been so different from everyone's at the table that he had no stories to tell. Hailey knew how it felt to be on the outside looking in, how lonely that could feel.

While her brother regaled them with his unfortunate encounter with a skunk—as opposed to Cam's skink—Hailey had taken Winn's hand beneath the table linen, linking her fingers with his.

"Where did Dad take the guys?" Anna set her cup down and removed a ball of buttercup-yellow yarn and two knitting needles from a tapestry bag next to her chair.

"Out to his shop," Kathy said, the needles in her hands already clicking as she added rows of perfect stitches to the cashmere christening blanket she was knitting for her grandbaby.

Though the word *dad* sounded strange coming from Anna's lips, it also sounded right. Hailey knew her parents had been pleased their daughter-in-law had recently agreed to call them Mom and Dad instead of Frank and Kathy.

An only child, Anna's parents had died when she'd been a freshman in college, victims of carbon-monoxide poisoning.

Hailey tried not to grimace when her mother brought out a ball of pea-green and gray variegated yarn and put it in front of her, telling her she should knit Winn a scarf.

Looking at the ugly yarn, Hailey couldn't quite decide if this meant her mother liked or hated Winn.

"Frank wanted to show Tripp the cradle he's building for our new grandchild." Though she smiled at Anna, Kathy's voice was strung tight as piano wire. "He thought about just presenting it to you both once it was done, but we felt he should show it to Tripp now, help him prepare, get his thoughts—and emotions—in order."

"I think that was smart," Anna said softly. Her green eyes held a hint of sorrow. "Gayle's death hit us all hard. But for Tripp, well, having me pregnant brings all those fears back. He tries to hide his worry, but—"

Kathy took Anna's hand and gave it a squeeze. "You're a midwife. You know what happened to Gayle is a rarity. If she'd have been near a large medical center—"

"I know," Anna interrupted. "I'm not the one who's worried."

Hailey wondered how it was going out in the shop. How

would her brother react to something so tangibly tied to the upcoming birth of his child?

The depth of pain her brother experienced when he'd lost his wife and their unborn child had shaken Hailey. Tripp had been living the dream. Until that moment, anything he ever wanted had been served up to him on a silver platter.

But he'd survived those dark days. Survived the horrific loss…and come out stronger. Now he had Anna. Though Hailey would never voice the thought, she believed Anna was a much better match for her family-oriented brother than Gayle had been.

"Have you started on the nursery?" Hailey asked, then instantly regretted the question when she saw Anna's face.

"Not yet," Anna said with an extrabright smile.

"Plenty of time." Kathy patted Anna's hand.

"I feel as if I've monopolized most of the conversation this evening." Anna looped a strand of yarn around one needle. "Hailey, we haven't even talked about you and Winn."

"Not much to say." Hailey took a sip of coffee. "I'm still watching Cam."

"What about the mistletoe?" her mother asked.

Hailey's smile froze on her lips. "What about it?"

"I was wondering if Mary Karen and Travis put it out this year." Her mother's innocent expression didn't fool her. "You girls made it sound like an annual tradition."

Hailey paused, remembering the mistletoe Winn had hung from the ceiling fan over his sofa.

"Lots and lots of mistletoe." Anna's laugh sounded girlish and carefree. The worry that had darkened her eyes moments before had disappeared. "Your son made it his mission to find every last sprig."

"That's my boy." Her mother shifted her teasing gaze. "How about you, Hailey? Did Winn kiss you under the mistletoe?"

Hailey's cheeks burned red hot. She saw her mother and Anna exchange a quick significant glance.

Kathy laughed. "I'll take that as a yes."

A kiss had only been the beginning. Thinking of everything she and Winn had done under the mistletoe did nothing to lessen Hailey's blush. If anything, remembering his touch brought more heat to her cheeks and an ache of longing deep in her belly.

She wanted Winn to hold her, touch her…love her as she loved him.

The realization brought both wonder and fear.

How had this happened? She hadn't been looking for love, hadn't wanted to find anyone special until her life was more settled. Yet, it had happened.

Anna continued to wrap yarn around her needle, casting one uniform stitch after another, while Hailey fumbled with hers.

"Tripp is impressed with Winn," Anna announced.

Kathy's smile encouraged her daughter-in-law to continue.

"Initially he wasn't sure what to think of him. On first impression, Winn can come across as being a chip off the old block." Anna cast an apologetic look at Hailey. "But after they talked at the party, Tripp is convinced he misjudged him. And you certainly seemed to like him."

"He makes me feel good about myself," Hailey murmured.

"I thought at first his paying so much attention to you was self-serving and some kind of act," Anna said, not appearing to notice Hailey's indrawn breath. "I don't think that anymore."

With lips pressed together, Hailey pulled out a series of loose stitches. She believed Winn to be sincere. She desperately wanted to believe he was sincere.

But she'd been duped before. Completely. Foolishly. And that knowledge was a heavy weight to bear.

* * *

Winn cast a sideways glance at Hailey. Though her hand rested comfortably in his as they walked, there was a distance between them that hadn't been there earlier.

He didn't understand what had caused it. From his perspective the evening had gone well. The snake had added a touch of levity leading to a lively conversation over dinner.

Winn had been astonished by the stories of skunks, skinks, possums and mischievous raccoons. Then, afterward, he'd been surprised when Frank had ushered them into a heated exterior building and uncovered a partially finished cradle.

At first it had been awkward to witness what he believed should have been a private moment between father and son. When Cam had begun jabbering about how cool it was and asking if that thing really rocked a baby, Winn had opened his mouth to silence the boy. But he'd caught Frank's look and shut his mouth without speaking.

The more Cam talked the more Tripp's tight expression eased, and the haunted look left his eyes.

By the time the cover was replaced over the cradle, Tripp was back to his normally jovial self. They discussed golf while helping Frank move an ancient table saw from one part of the shop to another corner.

On their way back to the house, Cam held Frank's hand and skipped beside the older man. That gave Tripp and Winn the opportunity to discuss some of the concerns about Winn's project that had been brought to the mayor's office.

But by far the best part of the evening had been being with Hailey: laughing with her, holding her hand beneath the dining room table and sharing a piece of what her mother called Heaven-and-Hell Cake. The multilayered cake was a decadent delight, containing both angel food and devil's food cake, peanut-butter mousse and milk-chocolate ganache.

He'd wanted to kiss the thin layer of mousse and ganache off Hailey's lips right there in front of everyone. Out of respect for her parents, he'd resisted. Besides, what he and Hailey shared was so new that he found himself wanting to hold the emotions close and savor them.

He'd been glad she hadn't wanted to head straight to her condo when they got home. Instead, she'd suggested a walk.

"Not so far ahead, Cam," Winn called out. "Stay in sight."

"Okay," the boy called back over his shoulder, retaining a tight hold on Bandit's leash.

"A walk was an excellent idea," Winn said to Hailey.

"Cam was revved after the time at the ranch." Hailey's gaze lingered on the little boy a quarter of a block ahead. A slight smile lifted her lips. "Not at all ready for bed."

"Which is surprising, considering how little sleep he got last night." Winn shook his head and chuckled. "Heck, how little sleep we all got."

Hailey stifled a yawn. "I could go to bed right now."

"Can I join you?"

She chuckled and gave his shoulder a shove. "You're always working the angles, Ferris."

"Like father like son."

Her smile faded.

"Hey." He closed his hand around hers. "What's wrong?"

"I was thinking of what Cam asked my dad."

Winn's expression tightened. "I'll speak with him later. I didn't want to make a big deal of it at the time. Especially with your father being so gracious to him."

Winn had been as shocked as Hailey when, shortly before they left the ranch, Cam had asked Frank if he could call him Grandpa. Just thinking of that moment brought a lump to Winn's throat.

Frank's voice had been thick and gravelly as he told Cam he'd be honored.

"Don't say anything to him, Winn." There was a pleading note in Hailey's voice he didn't understand. "Cam recently lost the only grandparents he's known. I mean, from what you've said, your father never did embrace that role."

"No." A chill, at odds with the warm summer night, washed over him. "He didn't. I don't believe that will change."

"Cam misses his grandparents."

The fact that she spoke the truth infuriated him. He wasn't angry with her but at the situation. Cam had endured so much loss.

"Do you think it's easy?" His words were low and tight with frustration. "The fact that I'm depriving him of grandparents he knows and loves?"

"Of course I don't think it's easy." Her tone, warm as a stiff shot of fine bourbon, soothed the raw spot in his heart. "Have you considered inviting them here?"

He slammed his brows together. "Why would I do that?"

"To let them see how happy he is here, how close the two of you are," she said, squeezing his hand. "Perhaps that would reassure them that Cam is right where he needs to be."

"I briefly considered that option," Winn admitted, but didn't tell her that the thought filled him with terror. He'd lost his son once. He couldn't bear to lose him again. Or have him hurt again.

"What are your reservations?"

Winn realized he was witnessing one of Hailey's greatest strengths, this ability to calmly and rationally discuss a difficult issue without resorting to histrionics or picking a side without all the facts. Skills Vanessa had never mastered.

"What if they take him?" he asked, voicing his deepest fear. He thought how easy it would be for the couple to spirit the boy away while on an outing. How hard it would be to get him back. "They want him. What's to stop them?"

Thankfully, she didn't mention the law. They both knew

that he'd eventually get Cam back, but not without further emotional trauma to the child.

"You could supervise the visit," Hailey suggested. "Or hire someone to observe from a distance and only intervene if they attempted to take Cam out of Jackson Hole."

"Are you suggesting I hire a bodyguard for the boy?"

"Well, that way his grandparents could take him to the park or out for pizza without us worrying. And, with someone watching, we'd be assured he was safe."

Winn wondered if she even noticed she'd said "we." Even if she hadn't, he had, and it made him feel not so alone in this battle.

"I'm not sure I can take the risk, small though it might be," he said honestly.

"Talk with Nick." Those beautiful eyes, the color of the Wyoming sky, bore into his. "But remember, Cam loves them, just like he loves you. Sometimes with love you have to take a risk."

Chapter Fifteen

The next morning, instead of driving, Winn walked from the condo to Nick's office in downtown Jackson. When he called at eight, he'd expected to wait several days for an appointment.

The assistant, a professional-sounding woman by the name of Esther, told him there had been a ten-o'clock cancellation and he could have that time slot.

Winn had agreed, even though it meant that Hailey would need to take Cam to the psychologist without him. He'd already spoken personally with Dr. Peter Allman about his concerns and Hailey knew Cam's history as well as he did.

Today Pete, or his new associate, Dr. Gallagher, would speak with Cam privately. Winn decided being there wasn't essential, except for moral support. He was confident Hailey could handle that task.

A series of melodious bells chimed as Winn pushed open the door to the stone-fronted building just off Broadway. Though much more casually appointed than the law firms he was used to in Atlanta, the gleaming bamboo flooring in a fossilized gray with charcoal-colored walls above cherry-wood cabinets bespoke a richness usually seen in only the top-notch firms of major cities.

The receptionist, a middle-aged woman with wavy brown hair and a friendly smile, looked up. "How may I help you, sir?"

"I have an appointment with Mr. Delacourt at—"

"What's this mister business?" Nick appeared in the doorway of an office down the hall. Tall and broad-shouldered, with dark hair, the attorney in a hand-tailored suit started down the corridor.

He reached Winn in several long strides, clasping his hand in a firm shake. "Can I get you some coffee? Double shot of espresso?"

"Thank you. I'm fine."

Once the office door shut behind them, Nick gestured to a burgundy tufted sofa in one side of the large office. Winn took a seat and Nick settled into a chair to his right.

After a few minutes of casual conversation about mutual friends and sports, Nick lifted a sleek MacBook from a side table and placed it on his lap. His gaze fixed on Winn, his dark eyes inscrutable. "Tell me what I can do for you."

"You'll need some background information, beginning with the fact that Cameron isn't my biological son." Briefly, Winn recounted his history with Vanessa and Cam, making sure not to leave anything out.

Nick kept his gaze focused on Winn even as his fingers flew across the keyboard. "I'm surprised she left you in the will as his guardian."

"I'm certain it was an oversight."

"Perhaps." Nick's gaze narrowed. "Do you want to keep the boy?"

"Of course," Winn said immediately, shocked by the question even though he realized Nick needed to ask it.

"Cam is my son in every way that matters. I never wanted to sever our relationship. That was Brandon's doing."

"You plan to legally adopt him."

"Yes."

Nick sat back. "Tell me about the grandparents."

"Larry and Jan Robinette are Brandon's mother and father." Winn kept his voice even, though emotions surged when he remembered their threats. "They made it clear they planned to fight for custody."

Nick's steely-eyed gaze was suddenly razor sharp. "When and how did they make it clear?"

"Cam stayed with them after Vanessa and Brandon were killed." Winn recalled the day he'd gone to their home to pick up his son. "They didn't want to turn him over to me, but the attorney they'd contacted had told them—"

"They'd already secured legal counsel at that time?" Nick interrupted.

"Apparently." The vise that held Winn's chest in a stranglehold tightened. "They said their attorney told them they had to comply. I know they plan on gaining custody of Cameron, asserting the boy is their flesh and blood not mine."

Winn waited for Nick to tell him not to be concerned because not only was he listed as guardian in the will, he'd been the only father Cam had known for six years.

Heaviness settled over Winn when the words weren't forthcoming.

"I'll need to do some research." Nick's gaze grew thoughtful. "I know the Georgia legislature passed a bill in the last few years making the state grandparent-friendly for visitation. I assume Brandon didn't have a will?"

"No."

"Did Vanessa include a Letter of Explanation with hers?"

Winn inclined his head. "What is that?"

"Parents are encouraged to leave a written explanation

as to why they chose the person named in the will to be the guardian of their minor children." Nick met Winn's gaze. "I encourage my clients to include the letter with their will, especially if they think a judge could have reason to question their choice."

"I don't believe there was such a letter."

"I'll check to be sure," Nick said.

Winn leaned over and reached into his briefcase, pulling out a file of papers. "This is everything I have."

Nick took the packet. "Have you been contacted recently? At breakfast it sounded as though a challenge to your guardianship was imminent."

"I haven't heard from their attorney. Not yet, anyway. But I received a text on Friday from a friend who still lives in Georgia. He was the one who initially introduced me to Vanessa and we've stayed friends." Winn pushed to his feet, too wound up to sit. He moved to the window and stared unseeing out into the sunlight. "Anthony wanted me to know he heard through the grapevine that the Robinettes definitely plan to pursue full custody."

"Your friend did you a favor." Nick gazed at the folder Winn had handed him. "I appreciate your thoroughness. Coming here before you're served with papers was a smart move. It's always best to be prepared."

Winn didn't feel prepared. He felt off balance and unsteady. "What factors will the judge consider when determining Cam's best interests?"

"His preference. Who can best meet his needs in terms of stability and continuity of care. Moral fitness of the guardian. The relationship between you and Cam." Nick smiled reassuringly at Winn. "The fact that Vanessa named you as guardian and never took you out of her will, even after discovering you weren't Cam's father, is very much in our favor."

"A custody battle will be hard on Cam." Winn grit his

teeth. "I'll never forgive Brandon's parents for adding to his turmoil."

"He *is* their grandson." Nick's tone was matter-of-fact. "It appears they've been an active part of his life the last two years."

Winn narrowed his gaze. "Whose side are you on?"

"Yours," Nick said promptly. "That's why I'd like you to at least consider reasonable visitation. We may be able to head off a full-blown court battle by making that relatively minor concession."

Relatively minor? Winn opened his mouth to say it'd be a cold day in hell before he'd let those people near his boy again, but instead he found himself confiding in Nick.

"Hailey actually suggested I invite them here for a visit. She said if they see how happy he is with me, perhaps they'll be less likely to sue for custody."

"Smart woman." Nick's lips quirked up. "Too bad she's only your temporary nanny and not your wife. I need to warn you, the fact that you're single may weigh against you."

Winn's heart dropped, but he refused to worry about his marital status. It was what it was. "As an attorney, do you believe allowing them access to Cam would be wise when everything is so up in the air?"

"It would definitely show goodwill, but I'd suggest having a child advocate with them on any outing where you're not present. I can get you names of ones the firm has used in the past." Nick rose to his feet. "I'll be in touch."

Winn left the office, his insides a mass of churning emotions. Not in the mood to think about the battle he might be facing and the detrimental effect on his son, Winn covered the distance to his condo in long, ground-covering strides. By the time he reached the steps leading to the second floor, the tightness bunching his shoulders had eased.

Yet he still didn't know what he was going to do.

Not about Cam and the boy's grandparents.

Not about his feelings for Hailey.

Life, he mused, had been easier when he had only business concerns to worry about.

Easier, he thought, but incredibly empty.

Hailey had listened intently to Winn's account of his meeting with Nick. As they discussed the pros and cons of giving Cam's grandparents access, she'd felt good about being included in the decision-making process. It showed Winn understood how much she cared about Cam and valued her opinion.

As she stood in front of Winn's door on Friday evening, she wondered when he was going to make a decision. She assumed he hadn't yet or she'd have heard. Wouldn't she?

Stop being ridiculous, she told herself. *You'd be the first person he'd tell.*

Hailey knew part of her sour mood stemmed from the last-minute summons, er, invitation, to a barbecue at Winn's father's ranch. Jim couldn't carve out an hour or two to see his grandson, but he obviously had time to host a party to introduce some new assistant he'd hired.

The worst part was, since Winn had to hire a sitter to watch Cam this evening, he'd regretfully bowed out of escorting Hailey to her friend's wedding tomorrow afternoon. Children weren't invited to the nuptials or the reception and Winn didn't want to leave Cam with a sitter two nights in a row.

Because Hailey would be helping Cassidy with the makeup for the wedding party, that meant she wouldn't get to see him or Cam at all tomorrow.

But it wasn't as if they didn't have plans already in place for Sunday—church followed by breakfast at the Coffee Pot. Encouraged, Hailey plastered on a bright smile and rapped on the door. By the time Winn answered her knock Hailey had shrugged off most of her melancholy.

Winn's eyes widened when he saw her. He let loose a

low whistle. "You look fresh as a summer parfait in that dress. I swear, you'll be the prettiest woman at the party."

His gaze lingered on the bodice of the white dress with tiny yellow flowers long enough to send blood humming through her veins.

"You don't look half-bad yourself." With a move that felt like second nature, Hailey stepped to Winn and he wrapped his arms around her.

She was lifting her face for a kiss, when she heard a throat being cleared. Hailey stiffened, realizing they had company.

Over Winn's shoulder, Hailey saw Kate Dennes staring at them with a bemused smile.

"Don't let me interrupt." Kate waved a perfectly manicured hand in the air. "Just keep it PG-rated, 'kay?"

"Spoilsport." Hailey brushed a chaste kiss against Winn's lips then took a step back and smiled warmly at Kate. She'd always liked the popular doctor. "I didn't know you were watching Cam this evening."

"I'm not. This is Chloe's first babysitting job since getting her certificate. She's still pretty young." Kate lowered her voice. "I thought it best if I stayed to observe."

Hailey glanced around. "Did Joel come, too?"

"He and Sam are enjoying male-bonding time at home." There was a warmth to Kate's voice, one that was always present when she spoke of her husband or children. "Preliminary plans were to play a rousing game of blocks followed by a walk in the woods."

"I assumed you'd be at the barbecue tonight."

"We were invited," Kate confirmed.

Hailey expected as much. Joel was a successful entrepreneur, while Kate was a prominent pediatrician. The couple was the type Jim liked to include on his guest list.

"Regrettably we had to decline." The mischievous gleam in Kate's eyes told a different story. "Chloe was so excited to watch Cam this evening."

Hailey glanced around for the dark-haired girl who was the spitting image of her beautiful mother. "Where is Chloe?"

"Building a Lego space station with Cam," Winn answered, then glanced at his black Hublot encircling his wrist.

Even though Winn was dressed simply in navy twill pants and an oxford shirt, the sight of him sent warmth coursing through Hailey's veins. She wished she could spend the evening with him and Cam.

"I guess we should take off." Hailey tried unsuccessfully not to sigh.

"You look adorable," Kate told her.

Hailey glanced down at her dress. Normally, in Jackson Hole, an invitation to a barbecue meant burgers, brauts and beer. But Jim Ferris didn't do casual or relaxed. Though there would be an abundance of delicious food and drink, any beer would be imported. Wine would be the drink of choice and the atmosphere would be just shy of formal.

That was why Hailey had not only worn a dress but paired it with strappy heeled sandals. She'd even taken the time to fix her hair into tousled curls around her shoulders.

Winn turned to Kate. "There're a few things I need to explain about Cam's routine—"

"I'd prefer you speak directly with Chloe," Kate interrupted. "I'm simply a silent observer."

Winn glanced at Hailey and she saw the question in his eyes.

"Go ahead." She waved him on. "I'll keep Kate company. Tell Cam I'll be in to say good-night in a second."

Winn leaned over and brushed a kiss across her mouth before leaving the room.

Hailey felt her cheeks warm under Kate's speculative gaze. "Winn is a very affectionate man."

"I never realized that before, but I can see it now." Kate

chuckled before her expression turned serious. "Are you watching Cam for the entire summer?"

Hailey didn't even blink at the change in subject. Winn and Cam did it to her all the time.

"I am and it's going way too fast. He's a great kid." Hailey would miss seeing Cam every day. "Winn already has him enrolled in a before- and after-school care program this fall."

"Wonderful," Kate murmured.

"Why wonderful?"

"Has Meg spoken with you?"

Hailey shook her head.

"She and I are planning a business venture." Kate's eyes danced with excitement. "We thought you might be interested in embarking on this exciting new project with us. You've done excellent work with the patients of mine that you've seen."

"That's kind of you to say." Hailey took a seat at one end of the sofa and Kate sat at the other end. "Tell me about this venture."

"We're building a multidisciplinary therapy clinic. The clinic will provide physical, occupational and speech therapy for children and adults."

"Meg already has her own physical-therapy clinic," Hailey said slowly. "And the hospital has OTs and STs on staff for outpatients."

"Meg plans to fold her practice into this endeavor. We've acquired a piece of land in the Spring Gulch business park, not far from Dr. Allman's new clinic. Joel will break ground on the building next week."

Apparently, Hailey's continued confusion must have shown because Kate continued. "Mitzi McGregor, Meg and I will be partners. As an orthopedic surgeon, Mitzi sees a need for a clinic that offers more accessible hours for patients. Eventually, if you're interested, you could buy into the practice."

Hailey's heart gave an excited leap. Working with Cam on his speech had only reinforced how much she loved her chosen profession. This sounded as if she'd be able to put in more hours doing what she loved.

"What do you think?" Kate asked after a few seconds had passed.

"If you're asking if I'd like to work for you, the answer is I would. But I do have some questions. Perhaps we can find a time to sit down and discuss the position in more detail?"

"Absolutely." Kate captured her hand and gave it a squeeze. "Any of the three of us can answer your questions. Just so you know, we'll be flexible regarding hours and—"

"Ready?" Winn asked, striding into the room.

"I'll give you a call tomorrow," Hailey told Kate.

"I look forward to it," Kate said with a pleased expression.

As Hailey floated into Cam's room to say good-night, all she could think of was what a difference a few minutes could make.

Chapter Sixteen

Hailey told Winn about her conversation with Kate as they left Jackson and drove to his father's ranch. The Tetons remained in the distance while they drove past subdivisions that seemed to rise out of nowhere. They'd then disappear to be replaced by vast expanses of grazing land.

"Are you interested?" he asked, his voice carefully neutral.

"Very interested." Happiness spilled from her voice. "The hours will be flexible. It sounds like if I ever needed to leave early on a Friday to help Cassidy, it wouldn't be a problem."

"They'd be lucky to have you."

"Thank you. But I haven't made a decision yet. And if it doesn't work for me, there are a lot of excellent speech therapists in the area."

"Not with your warmth and caring and talent," Winn argued.

Hailey touched his arm. "That's sweet."

"It's the truth," he insisted with obvious sincerity.

He was, she realized, one of her biggest champions.

"If they need you to start before the end of the summer, I can make other—"

"No worries," Hailey said before he could say more. "They haven't even broken ground."

She forced a smile at odds with the sudden heavy feeling in her chest. "I'm afraid you and Cam are stuck with me for the duration. I mean, until the end of the summer."

"The duration sounds better." He shot her a wink then shut off the engine and stepped out of the car, rounding the front to open her door.

The windows of his father's extravagantly expensive ranch home gleamed like jewels in the soft summer night. Even from the end of the driveway, where they'd been forced to park, sounds of music and laughter spilled from the house.

Hailey tilted her head and listened. "First time I've heard jazz played at a barbecue."

Winn grinned. "Dad always has set his own entertainment rules."

"Something tells me tonight is going to be full of surprises." She slipped her arm through his, wanting the physical closeness, even if it was only during the short walk to the door. "Who'd your father hire, anyway? I don't think you told me the person's name."

"That's because I don't know it." Winn covered her hand with his as he meandered toward the house, his steps as slow and plodding as hers on this lazy summer night.

It was as if neither of them wanted this time alone to end.

"Whoever it is, I feel sorry for the poor bastard."

Hailey bit back a smile. "That's not very nice."

"It's true." Winn lifted a shoulder in a shrug. "The new one won't last longer than any of the others. My dad is a real SOB. He goes through assistants like he goes through a bottle of bourbon."

Hailey cast a sideways glance, hearing the simmering

anger beneath the carelessly tossed words. Something told her the intensity of his annoyance wasn't about an impromptu party fouling up their plans for tomorrow, or the fact Jim had hired a new assistant and was playing cat and mouse with the name.

"You're irritated he hasn't wanted to see Cam. That he puts you off when you try to schedule a time to get together."

Winn stopped at the base of the steps leading to the house. There was a cold fury in his eyes now. But it was the momentary flash of pain she'd seen that made her heart ache.

"Do you know what he told me?" Winn stepped away from her, agitation fueling his movements. "He said Cam isn't really his grandson, so he'd prefer *the boy* call him Mr. Ferris."

Winn swore and raked a hand through his hair. It was a nervous gesture from a man who prided himself on being perfectly groomed, no matter what the circumstances.

At any other time, the tufts of his thick dark hair sticking up at odd angles would have made her smile. Not tonight. Winn had spoken the truth. Jim Ferris really was an SOB.

Only the fact that he was Winn's father, and she didn't want to escalate the tension between him and his dad even further, kept Hailey's tone even. "Doesn't he realize the love binding you and Cam together is stronger than blood?"

"I don't believe my father knows what love is." Weariness settled over Winn's handsome features. "I don't even know why I came tonight."

"So you can say you've listened to jazz at a Jackson Hole barbecue." Hailey forced a cheery tone. Reaching up, she smoothed his hair in a gesture that halfway through struck her as a little too wifely. She dropped her hand. "There. You're perfect."

He was, she thought with a sigh, perfect for her. The only trouble was, *she'd* never been perfect for anyone.

Winn captured her hand. "We won't stay long. I promise."

"It's your call."

"Don't leave me, Hailey." His fingers tightened around hers. "I couldn't bear it."

"Oh, look." Relief flooded her as she saw Jim Ferris step onto the porch. "There's your father."

Thirty minutes later, Hailey eyed the door longingly as one of the many bartenders stationed throughout the sprawling ranch house mixed her a Crazy Coyote Margarita. Anna and her mother had raved about the taste of the drink for months, so Hailey had decided to give it a try.

As a lime wedge was added to the salt-rimmed glass, Hailey regretted her earlier response to Winn. If she could go back in time, she'd have whispered something suggestive in Winn's ear before they'd reached the door. Something X-rated, guaranteed to make him sweep her into his arms and head back to the car.

That way, she wouldn't have had to endure Jim's effusive and obviously phony welcome, complete with a hug. She wouldn't have to endure this boring party, where one minute felt like ten. And more important, she'd never have been faced with seeing Josh Gratzke again. What were the odds the man who'd used her would end up being Jim's new assistant? Of course, after her brother had given him the boot, there probably hadn't been many doors open to him in Jackson Hole.

"Looks like you landed on your feet."

Hailey stifled a groan, immediately recognizing Josh's voice with its almost imperceptible lisp. Her mission to avoid Josh all evening had come to a swift end. It figured he'd wait until Winn was engaged in a serious conversation with Merle Bach, a board of trustees member, to approach her.

"Here you go, miss." The college-age bartender handed her the drink, flashing a warm smile. "One Crazy Coyote."

Despite feeling Josh's eyes boring into her, Hailey ignored him and took a big sip of her freshly made drink, blinking at the strong taste of tequila.

"Margaritas are such a girlie drink."

Like a bothersome mosquito, he obviously wasn't going away without a couple of swift swats.

"Were you speaking to me?" she asked, gazing at him over the rim of her glass.

She had to admit he fit in with tonight's crowd in his gray pants and charcoal-colored shirt. But he was too skinny, his lanky frame more like a boy's than a man's. And his eyes had a beady, ratlike quality that she'd never noticed before. She wondered how she'd ever thought him attractive.

"Just wanted to be social and say hello." He offered her one of those lazy smiles she once thought so charming.

Of course, that was before she'd seen him for what he was…a slimy reptile, far more dangerous than any three-foot garter.

"I do believe you've been avoiding me." His gaze drifted over her in an almost intimate appraisal.

In that moment she found herself incredibly glad she'd never slept with him.

"Avoiding you would presume you matter to me." She sipped her drink, pausing for effect. "You don't."

"Ouch." He placed a hand to his heart. "You wound me, sweetheart."

"I'm not your sweetheart. Never was." She waved a hand carelessly in the air. "Oh, congrats on the new position. I think you and Jim will be very happy together. Two peas in a slime pod and all that…"

He gave an incredulous laugh. "You're still steamed about that little thing with your brother."

"Are you referring to how you used me to get in good with Tripp?"

"It was business." A puzzled look crept into his eyes. "I

didn't do anything different than Ferris is doing now. You don't seem upset with him."

Hailey pulled her brows together. The alcohol must be affecting her more than she realized, because Josh wasn't making any sense. "Jim Ferris isn't using me to get to my brother."

"Didn't say he was, although I'm sure he reserves that option for the future." Josh clucked his tongue. "I was speaking of his son. Winn is the one using you for his own purposes."

"Good try." Hailey could have cheered when the words came out casual and offhand—and hopefully just a little bit bored.

"In case you haven't noticed, Jim has been a whole lot nicer to you than he's been to most of his other guests." Josh lifted his glass of beer but paused before taking a sip, his eyes sharp and assessing on her face. "Why do you think that is?"

Hailey had noticed Jim's fawning but had assumed Winn had put his father on notice. Perhaps the old man had something up his sleeve. That didn't mean she'd fall for whatever he had planned. Or that Winn had anything to do with the scheme.

Josh was simply fishing.

"Believe what you want." Hailey stole a furtive glance in Winn's direction, dismayed to find him still in intense conversation with Merle.

With the vote on the development only days away, Merle—and her brother —were swing votes. Although, the last time she'd spoken with Tripp, he now stood firmly behind Winn's project.

"Winn is a pro," Josh said admiringly, following the direction of her gaze. "Like father like son."

Hailey wasn't sure what he meant and she didn't care. "I'm bored with this conversation."

"If you're angry at me, you should be with him, too," Josh insisted when she turned to leave.

Despite her gut telling her to keep walking, Hailey paused.

"I overheard Jim on the phone the other day, laughing and telling his son he's a chip off the old block." Josh's gaze sharpened when she flinched. "And while Jim isn't keen on kids, Winn keeping the boy turned out to be a smart move because it not only gave him a way to cozy up to you and get his project approved, if he marries you it'll make the custody fight a slam dunk."

Hailey felt as if the air had been knocked from her lungs. But she refused to give Josh the satisfaction of knowing his remarks had knocked her slightly off balance.

She trusted Winn. She had no reason not to trust him.

Lifting her lips in what she hoped was a sly smile, Hailey mused aloud. "Since Jim and I *are* so tight, I believe I'll just stroll over and confirm what you told me is true."

Josh blanched but rallied with a laugh. "He'll just deny it."

This time the smile that blossomed on her lips was genuine. "Perhaps. But he'd know you said it. I believe that alone will secure your spot in the unemployment line."

Though Hailey had no intention of initiating a conversation with Winn's father, she liked seeing fear chase away the smugness in Josh's eyes.

"Looks like Jim is finishing up his conversation with one of the trustees."

She'd only taken a couple of steps when Josh's hand shot out, his fingers digging hard into her wrist.

"You're not going anywhere." Josh's tone was low and so menacing a shiver slithered up her spine.

Her breath came in short puffs, but when she spoke her voice was steady. "Take your hand off me."

"You best do as the lady asks." Liam Gallagher, her

high-school friend, stepped forward to stand by Hailey. His unwavering gaze pinned Josh.

Though dressed like a gentleman in brown chinos and an ivory shirt, Liam gave the impression of a man you didn't want to cross.

"Hey." Josh lifted both hands, that phony smile returning to his lips. "I don't want any trouble."

Hailey pinned Josh with a steely glare. "Don't come near me again or I *will* go to Jim."

"You deserve what you get," Josh volleyed back before melting into the crowd.

More shaken than she wanted to admit, Hailey turned to Liam and flashed a bright smile. "I didn't even realize you'd be here. But I'm glad you are."

Hailey started talking about the party, the decorations and the food. The people she knew who were here and those who weren't. She was chattering, practically babbling, as emotions had her insides pitching like a small vessel in storm-tossed seas.

"Who was that guy?" Liam demanded, his gaze focused in the direction where Josh had disappeared.

"He's not important. I believe I need some fresh air." Hailey gazed up at him and smiled beguilingly. "And another margarita, please."

"You're easy to please." The tension left Liam's face and he returned her smile. Moments later, with drink in hand, Hailey stepped out onto the flagstone patio and let the warm night air slide over her. But it did little to heat the coldness that had gone straight to her bones.

Hailey took a sip of her Crazy Coyote, the gentle breeze ruffling her hair.

"What was going on back there?" Liam asked in the same conversational tone he undoubtedly used with his clients. "You looked ready to deck the guy."

When she didn't immediately answer, his gaze searched

hers and she saw worry reflected in the chocolate depths of his eyes.

She felt a surge of warmth. Liam was a friend. And he'd never used her. Of that she was certain. "Look at you, all grown-up and handsome."

"I don't know about that," he said with an easy smile, "but I do know you're the prettiest woman here."

The words were so similar to the ones Winn had uttered earlier that Hailey's smile faded. What Josh had said couldn't be true. Winn despised his dad. He wouldn't be in league with him.

He also knew how badly Josh had hurt her. He wasn't callous enough to follow in the jerk's footsteps. Winn wasn't callous at all. He was kind. Generous. Full of love.

Tears sprang to her eyes but she blinked them back before Liam could notice. She moved to the edge of the patio and gazed up at the moon.

Liam joined her, placing his glass on a wrought-iron patio table. Despite her efforts to control her rioting emotions, he appeared to sense her despair. He tipped up her chin with gentle fingers. "Tell me what's wrong, Hailey. I want to help."

"There you are. I've been looking—"

Hailey jerked her head in the direction of Winn's voice just in time to see his smile disappear.

Liam's hand slowly dropped to his side. At the murderous look in Winn's eyes, he took a step back but remained at Hailey's side.

"Winn." Hailey attempted to swallow around the sudden dryness in her throat. When that didn't work, she took a big drink of her margarita before she tried again. "I'd like you to meet an old friend of mine."

Winn's face was cold and austere. If looks could kill, Liam would be six feet under right now.

"Winston Ferris, this is Dr. Liam Gallagher. He and I went to high—"

"I know who he is, Hailey. He's the psychologist who has been seeing Cam," Winn interrupted.

A warm smile blanketed Liam's face and he extended his hand. "He's a wonderful boy."

For a second, Winn only stared at Liam's extended hand. Then he gave it a perfunctory shake.

Nervous energy replaced the blood in Hailey's veins. She experienced an almost uncontrollable urge to giggle. Not that she saw anything funny about the situation. Quite the contrary.

"So you and Hailey are old friends." Despite the coolness in his eyes, Winn looped a proprietary arm around her shoulders. The gesture saying quite clearly, "She is mine."

Normally Hailey would have welcomed the gesture. Now she stiffened, remembering Josh's words. Had she been played for a fool once again?

"Hailey and I dated in high school." Liam shot her a fond smile. "She was my first love."

A tiny muscle in Winn's jaw jumped.

"First love?" Hailey scoffed, a nervous giggle slipping past frozen lips. "We went steady for all of three months."

"An eternity to a sixteen-year-old boy." Liam grinned good-naturedly. "Be careful of this one, Ferris. She'll break your heart and ten years later won't even remember you."

"Stop."

Liam's teasing smile disappeared at her tone's sharp edge.

"He knows I'm joking, Hailey. Right, Winn?"

Winn gave a curt nod, and an awkward silence descended.

Liam rocked back on his heels. "If you decide you'd like to slip in a session for Cam after his grandparents leave next week, I'll be happy to fit him in."

Hailey whirled, the movement dislodging Winn's arm from her shoulders. "Cam's grandparents are coming to Jackson?"

Winn shifted uncomfortably. "Plans are for them to fly in on the third and stay until the fifth."

"When were you going to tell me?" Hurt snaked its way around her heart. Why hadn't Winn said anything to her?

"Ah." Liam pulled out his cell phone and held it up, though neither of them was paying him much attention. "Excuse me. I need to make a call. Nice to see you, Winn. Good seeing you again, Hailey."

Liam was already backing up. Apparently a man with a PhD in child psychology knew when retreat was the best option.

Hailey was glad to see him go. There was so much she needed to say to Winn. The trouble was, now that they were alone, her thoughts were such a tangled mess she wasn't sure where to begin. Perhaps the second Crazy Coyote had been a mistake.

"It appears you and Liam have decided to renew your... friendship."

It took her a while to catch on to what he was implying.

"Oh, that's rich." Hailey slammed her now empty margarita glass on the patio table, the movement making her sway slightly. "You're trying to turn this on me so I won't see what's going on. Let me tell you right now. It. Won't. Work."

His brows pulled together as if she was speaking an unfamiliar language. He cast a hand in the direction of the empty glass. "How many of those have you had tonight?"

"You know how many?" Her voice rose menacingly as she took a step closer. Putting both hands against his chest and giving him a not-so-gentle shove. "Not nearly enough. You...you jerk."

Her head swam, but she had herself focus. "When were you going to tell me about Cam's grandparents?"

"Nick only got back to me with the confirmation this afternoon," Winn protested, looking puzzled at her irritation. "I'm still undecided if having them come is a good thing or not. That's why I didn't say anything. There's still time to cancel."

"If you're not saying anything, how did Liam know?"

Winn's gaze never wavered from her face. "We talked about it after Cam's session yesterday. I thought it'd be best for Dr. Gallagher to know their arrival was a possibility."

Hailey put a hand to her head. Maybe his explanation made sense. But then she thought about what Josh had said.

"What other things haven't you told me?" Her breath came hard and fast as if she was nearing the end of a race, headed for a finish line she'd never wanted to cross.

Confusion blanketed his face. "Nothing. I've been straight with you."

"How about the con you and your father have going? The one I fell for—hook, line and sinker."

Warily, he stepped closer. "My father and I don't have any con going on."

"Not according to Josh." She slapped a hand to her forehead and swayed again. "I'm such a sap."

A muscle in Winn's jaw jumped. "You'd actually believe anything that sniveling weasel has to say?"

"He is a weasel, but he makes sense." Her laugh ended on a sob. But when Winn stepped forward, concern etching his brow, she held up a hand and shook her head in warning.

"Tell me what Josh said." Winn's voice was quiet, but his tone brooked no argument.

"Why?" she cried out. "So you can deny it? Explain it away?"

Winn raked his hand through his hair, frustration evident in the movement. "So I can clarify any misunderstanding."

"My head is swimming. I'm not sure I can process this right now." Tears stung the backs of her eyes. She blinked rapidly and rubbed her temples, wishing again she hadn't chugged that second Coyote. "I need to stop and think. But I can't think."

"Hailey, let me explain."

She started and kept walking, only stopping when she reached the door to turn back. "I don't know if I can trust you."

"If you walk away now we may never get this fixed."

"I don't even know if there is anything to fix," she told him honestly. "I just don't know."

The alcohol allowed all the fears and worries she'd tried to ignore to rise to the surface. From everything she'd observed with her friends, the course of true love usually hit a few boulders. But with Winn, the path had been smooth. Too smooth?

Though she wished she could take his words at face value, Hailey worried she was missing something. If Josh was right and Winn was using her, this time her heart wouldn't simply be bruised, it would be broken.

Chapter Seventeen

When Winn arrived home, Cam was already in bed. Kate and Chloe were at the kitchen table playing a board game.

"You're home early." Kate's smile faded and Winn realized he wasn't doing a very good job of hiding his emotions. She pushed back her chair and stood. "Is something wrong?"

"Nothing that can't be fixed," he muttered. He *would* get to the bottom of what had happened between him and Hailey this evening. He had to be missing something, because Hailey's behavior didn't make sense.

Chloe busied herself picking up the pieces of the game and putting them back in the box.

Two lines formed between Kate's brows. "Is there anything I can do to help?"

Winn shook his head then flashed a smile that felt foreign on his lips. "How was Cam for you?"

Kate's eyes were too sharp and her expression too sympathetic. Right now, he had to hold on to his anger at whoever and whatever had caused Hailey to doubt his feelings for her.

"Ah, Mr. Ferris."

Grateful for the distraction, Winn focused his attention on Chloe.

"Cameron was a good boy," the girl reported in a tone that reminded him of Mrs. Burk, his third-grade teacher. "We played with Lego and then with his trucks."

From the way her nose crinkled, Winn discerned Tonka trucks weren't high on her list of fun activities.

"We watched a movie, then he had a snack." The teenager, the spitting image of her dark-haired mother, consulted a notepad. "Cameron was in bed at nine and asleep by nine-fifteen."

Winn didn't care what time his son had fallen asleep. Right now he was just glad that once Kate and Chloe left, he could pour himself a stiff drink and try to figure out what had happened tonight.

"Thank you, Chloe. You did a fine job." He pulled out his wallet and handed her a couple of bills.

Her eyes widened when she saw the amount. "Wow. But this is too much. I only charge—"

"Keep it," Winn said abruptly, then softened his tone. "I appreciate you filling in on such short notice."

"Thank you, Mr. Ferris." Her sweet young face glowed. "Please call me again."

"You'll definitely be hearing from me." Winn shifted his gaze to Kate as they walked to the door. "It was good to see you again."

"Winn." Kate touched his sleeve, keeping her voice low, though there was really no need. Chloe had already put on her earbuds and was listening to music. "If there's anything Joel or I can do—"

"Thank you."

"Both you and Hailey mean a lot to us."

So much for keeping secrets, Winn thought. But her

offer touched him. Of all the places he'd ever lived, Jackson Hole was the only place that felt like home. And Hailey was the only woman he would ever love.

That was why he had to solve this mystery and make things right between them. Because when everything you wanted was within reach, failure wasn't an option.

Winn was at his father's door at 9:00 a.m. He'd called ahead and told his dad he needed to speak with him and he'd be right over.

Upon their arrival, he'd asked Elena to take Cam to the pond on the southern edge of the property to see the ducks. She'd immediately spirited Cam away.

"You could have at least let her stay long enough to get you some coffee," Jim groused.

His father must have a meeting scheduled for the morning, because his suit coat was on and gold cuff links winked just above his wrists.

"I'm capable of getting my own coffee," Winn informed his father. "And I didn't come to socialize."

"You made that clear." A look of displeasure crossed his father's face. "You have to speak to me about an urgent matter. Well, make it quick. My schedule is full and—"

"Tell me what you said to Josh about Hailey and me," Winn interrupted, his voice sharp enough to slice steel.

"I don't discuss personal matters with my assistant." Jim lifted a hand in a dismissive wave. "You should know that. Now, if that's all, I—"

"That's not all. Sit down," he snapped when his father began to rise.

Perhaps it was the look in Winn's eyes or the edge in his voice, but his father complied.

"I don't appreciate your tone, boy."

"I don't appreciate you screwing with my personal life." Winn's tone had his father's eyes widening. "Tell me everything you said to Josh."

Jim hesitated for so long Winn had to fight the urge to lunge across the table and wrap his hands around his neck.

"I may have mentioned that you cozying up to the mayor's sister was a smart move." Jim appeared to deliberately take his time lifting the mug of coffee to his lips. "That's all."

Winn's gaze slid over his father's face. Over the years he'd become somewhat of an expert at reading expressions. His gut said this was the truth. Still, he pressed. "Was anything said about a con?"

Puzzlement slithered across his father's face. "A con? No."

Winn pushed back his chair and stood. "I'll need Josh's address. And he's off your payroll as of today."

Jim's eyes flashed, his brows pulling together like two dark thunderclouds. "You're not in charge. You don't get to tell me who I can have on staff."

"In case you've forgotten, Granddad and I together have controlling interest in Ferris Inc. Push comes to shove, he'll side with me on this." Winn met his father's rigid gaze with an implacable one of his own. "I won't mess with the company if you get rid of your assistant. It's a small price to pay."

Jim's anger seemed to deflate like an untied balloon. He chuckled and shrugged. "Assistants are a dime a dozen, anyway. What did this one do to get you so riled?"

Winn's lips set in a thin hard line. "Let's just say no one screws with Winn Ferris and gets away with it."

"That kind of talk makes a father proud."

Winn gave a disgusted snort and headed out the backdoor to round up Cam.

A call from Meg on the way back into town had Winn making a detour to the Lassisters' mountain home.

Despite Josh's address burning a hole in his pocket,

Winn had known he couldn't take Cam with him when he confronted Josh.

Cam was excited to see Charlie, even more excited when he was asked to spend the night. Winn thought of what had happened the last time Cam had spent the night.

But before he could decline the offer, Cole put a hand on his shoulder and said in a low tone that the past shouldn't determine the future. He urged Winn to give the boy another chance.

Winn agreed to let Cam stay, and thought about what Cole had said on the drive to Josh's downtown apartment.

He acknowledged that his response last night had been driven by what had happened with Vanessa and Brandon. Liam had also been Hailey's first love.

The shock of finding her with the psychologist, his hands on her, had brought out old fears. But Hailey wasn't like Vanessa, he reminded himself. In the time they'd been together he'd learned Hailey wasn't capable of such subterfuge.

He owed her an apology.

That could wait, he decided. Until after he and Josh had a talk.

Josh opened the door to his apartment and Winn brushed past him into the small efficiency without speaking. Since it was Saturday, he thought he'd find the man at home.

"Hey," Josh protested. "I didn't invite you inside."

It was almost eleven and Josh wasn't even dressed for the day, Winn thought with disgust, eyeing the man's rumpled pajama bottoms and T-shirt.

Winn strode to the middle of the living room and turned, planting his feet. "Tell me what you said to Hailey last night."

The words were spoken as an order, one that Josh didn't appear to take seriously. With an insolent smile on his face, he strolled to the refrigerator. After getting a bottle of water for himself, he leaned against the counter. "Hailey and I used to date. We had a lot to say to each other."

"Don't screw with me, Gratzke." Winn clenched his hands into fists at his sides. "You made it sound as if I had some sort of con going with my father."

"If you know so much," Josh sneered, "why do you need me?"

"You're right," Winn said. "This is a waste of my time. You're a waste of my time."

"Glad I could be of assistance." Josh's voice was laced with sarcasm. "Hope I didn't mess things up with you and the babe. She's a hot little number. Given a little more time, I'd have gotten her into—"

Winn's right fist shot out, connecting solidly with Josh's eye. He gave a yelp of pain and staggered back.

"That hot little number is my future wife, you little weasel." Winn strolled to the door, turned and paused with his hand on the knob. "By the way, you're fired."

"You can't fire me."

"Oh, I can. And I just did." Winn smiled faintly. "It appears my father forgot to mention that ours is a family-owned business and I control the majority of the shares."

Winn pulled the door shut behind him with a firm thud.

Future wife?

Winn's thoughts drifted to Hailey. He'd never known such a beautiful, smart and caring woman. She made him a better person. She made him happy. He couldn't imagine his life without her in it.

The words he'd uttered had come from the heart. He loved Hailey. He wanted her to be his wife.

Now he needed to make sure she knew it, too.

Weddings normally made Hailey feel gooey and romantic inside. Today all she felt was depressed. The happy face she'd painted on this morning was in serious danger of slipping.

There was only so much gushing she could take about love and romance and happily-ever-after. The sad thing was, only twenty-four hours earlier, she'd been having all those happy thoughts about Winn.

Not anymore.

Tears sprang to her eyes, but she blinked them back and focused her attention on transforming Karla Anderson, her high-school friend, into the most beautiful bride ever.

She'd done the makeup for Karla's six attendants, all family members, before focusing on the bride.

"I've got to quit yammering." Karla's cheeks turned a dusky pink. "It's just that I'm so happy...when I once never thought I'd be."

Hailey wasn't sure how to respond. She knew Karla's complicated history with her fiancé, Justin. She remembered when Karla had fled to Jackson Hole from Kansas City.

Justin and she had broken up and he'd gone back to his old girlfriend around the time Karla had discovered she was pregnant. Though he'd begged her to get back together, she'd refused. It wasn't until after their baby was stillborn that they'd begun to mend their shattered relationship.

Now, a year later, they were getting married.

"I'm happy things worked out for you," Hailey said, and she meant it. "He loves you, Karla. I see it in his eyes whenever he looks at you."

"Learning to trust each other wasn't easy." Karla twisted a lace-embroidered handkerchief between her fingers. "We'd said some pretty hurtful—and unfair—things to each other. But we learned from our mistakes."

Karla's words hit a little too close to home.

Trust was at the heart of what had happened between her and Winn at the party. Hailey thought of the accusations she'd leveled at him. Accusations flung out in fear. Fear that she'd fallen in love with someone who could be using her.

She wanted to trust Winn. Deep down she believed he was someone she could trust. But what if she was wrong?

Hailey busied herself with the makeup, desperately wanting to change the subject. "Which one of these shades do you like best?"

"Hmm." Karla chewed on her lip as they studied the palate Hailey had thrust before her. "You're the expert."

"I think if we put this gold shadow on your lids, and use a violet or cranberry as a highlight, the green in your eyes will pop."

"Let's go for it." Her friend lifted her admiring gaze to Hailey. "How is it you always know the right thing to do?"

If only that were true…

Hailey's heart swelled, the pain making breathing difficult.

"What lipstick are you going to use?" Karla asked.

One step in front of the other, Hailey reminded herself. That's the only way she would get through the day.

"Mauve. Paired with the eye shadow colors we've selected, your skin will glow."

Securing the smile back on her lips, Hailey picked up the palate and went to work to transform her friend into a beautiful bride.

Winn didn't let a lack of an invitation stop him from attending the wedding of two people he'd never met. Besides, as far as he knew, Hailey had never retracted her invitation for him to be her plus one.

He hadn't been sure of the proper attire for an afternoon wedding in Jackson Hole but figured he couldn't go wrong with dark pants and a white shirt. He left his jacket in the car when he didn't see anyone else wearing one.

Thinking about clothing was only a distraction. His future happiness was at stake and he couldn't blow it.

Way to put the pressure on yourself, Ferris.

He told himself even if he couldn't convince Hailey of his veracity and sincerity tonight, he wouldn't give up. Eventually, he *would* make her see she could trust him.

Winn strolled into the church with several last-minute stragglers and found a seat in the back row.

When the bride entered, he stood with the rest of the guests and scanned the crowd for Hailey. Though he knew she was here—likely sitting with Cassidy—he hadn't been able to spot them. Winn tried looking for unusual shades of hair, not knowing what Cassidy would have chosen for today's festivities, but didn't see any out-of-the-ordinary colors.

Staying behind to make sure Karla's face was picture-perfect, Hailey watched with pride as her friend started down the aisle toward her waiting groom.

She waited until Karla was all the way down the aisle and standing beside Justin before searching for a seat.

Cassidy had promised to save a place beside her, but the church was so packed, Hailey was certain that hadn't been possible. She scanned the last few pews in case there was a spot open.

Her breath caught in her throat.

Winn.

She was certain she hadn't said his name aloud, but he turned and his eyes locked with hers.

No. She couldn't handle this. Not now.

For a second, she stood there, her feet heavy and un-moving, as if rooted in concrete. After giving three solid knocks against her ribs, her heart launched into an unsteady rhythm that made her light-headed.

Hailey whirled and began to run, rushing through a side door and into the bright sunshine. She couldn't speak with him. Not now. Any future conversations between them needed to be adult and rational. Right now her emotions were too close to the surface.

She slipped around the corner of the church and rested her back against the building, her breath coming in fast puffs. Shutting her eyes against the glare of the sun, she focused on slowing her breathing and her thoughts.

"Hailey." A warm hand closed around her arm.

Resisting the impulse to jerk away—which would have been childish—Hailey opened her eyes with a resigned sigh.

"Are you okay?" A frown furrowed Winn's brow.

"Just peachy. Why wouldn't I be?" she heard herself say. If using the word *peachy* in a sentence wasn't horrible enough, her voice broke on the last word.

To his credit, Winn pretended not to notice either occurrence, though the lines edging his eyes deepened.

"Come with me. Let's sit for a minute." He gestured with his head toward a heavily lacquered deacon's bench sitting beneath a large oak.

"I should get back to the ceremony," Hailey said vaguely.

"I doubt they'll miss either of us." He flashed a grin then sobered. "A few minutes of your time. Please."

Perhaps it was the *please.* Hailey couldn't be sure. Her brain was operating on some sort of auxiliary power.

She crossed the lawn in her blue silk dress, her heels digging into the soft earth, Winn silent beside her.

He didn't attempt to take her arm or touch her. That was good, she told herself. She needed to stay strong.

He waited for her to take a seat then settled beside her. "About last night—"

"Tell me something." Hailey swiveled, her gaze pinning him. Though running into him unexpectedly meant she was forced to wing it, she refused to let Winn control the conversation. "Why didn't you let me know you'd invited Cam's grandparents to Jackson Hole?"

"I'm so used to handling things on my own that I

plunged ahead. No. That's not correct. If the move back-fired, I wanted the onus to be on me."

"Not because I encouraged you."

"It was my decision," he repeated, his gaze steady. "Only mine."

They both knew she had been the one to first suggest then encourage the contact. Yet Winn appeared determined to take total responsibility for the outcome.

"Okay," she said. "Understood."

And Hailey did understand. He'd been trying to protect her.

Winn reached out, then appeared to think better of it and pressed his palms against his thighs instead. "I owe you another apology."

Recalling the rest of Josh's words brought a weary heaviness back to Hailey's heart.

"It was wrong to be jealous of you and Liam. It's just that you used to date him and…" Winn paused and shook his head, as if finding his thoughts jumbled and in need of clearing. "It's my hang-up and I put it on you. I'm sorry. You're not Vanessa. You're honest and I know I can trust you."

She tried to hold them back, truly she did, but despite her best efforts, two fat tears slipped down her cheeks.

Wuss, she chastised herself. *You have all these questions and, instead of asking them, you're going to sit here and* cry?

Hailey swiped at the tears. Having an adult conversation meant being honest. Tears were a sign of honest emotions. Her words needed to be equally forthright.

"Josh said you and your dad had a con going. That you were using me to get to Tripp."

Winn reached out and took her hand, resisting her attempts to pull away. "Why would I need to use you to get access to your brother? He's a public official with an open-door policy. And if you believe Tripp would vote based on a personal relationship, you don't know him as well as I thought you did."

For the first time Hailey could see the differences between Josh's and Winn's situations. Josh had wanted to secure a position in Tripp's office. Winn didn't need her to get close to Tripp. She experienced a tiny surge of hope. Then she remembered something else Josh had said. "Would you have a better chance of gaining custody of Cam if you were married?"

"Probably, but since I'm not married, it isn't a factor." Winn's gaze searched her face. "That's the truth, Hailey."

"But Josh—"

"Josh is a lying weasel." Winn spat the words. "If I could replay this morning, I'd punch him in the mouth rather than the eye."

"You hit him?"

"He had it coming." Winn's jaw jutted out, daring her to disagree.

Hailey smiled. "Is it wrong that I'm glad you hit him?"

"I sure don't regret it," he admitted. "Other than my hitting him did a number on my knuckles."

"Let me see." She lifted his hand then kissed the bruised, swollen flesh. "I'm sorry, Winn. I shouldn't have jumped so quickly to the wrong conclusions. Being so worried about someone using me is *my* hang-up. And I put it on you."

"We're quite the pair."

Hailey's laugh was rueful. "Yeah, quite the pair."

"Perfectly matched." Winn caressed her face with the back of his hand. "I love you, Hailey Randall."

"I love you, Winston Ferris." Her heart was in her throat, making her voice thick with emotion. "And I love Cam. I want us to be a family. All three of us."

Winn pulled her close as the bells began to peel and the bride and groom, along with their wedding party and guests, spilled from the church. He smiled. "That'll be us someday."

"Happy and in love?" Hailey kissed him full on the mouth. "We're already there."

Chapter Eighteen

"He won't ask me to marry him, Cass." Hailey blew out an exasperated breath, twirling one way and then the other in her friend's brightly colored salon chair.

Cassidy had been ringing up the last customer when Hailey arrived. The closed sign was now on the door and would remain there through tomorrow, the Fourth of July.

Jackson Hole citizens loved their holidays and Independence Day was no exception. For twenty-four hours the area was one big party, with activities for kids of all ages ending with a huge fireworks display over Snow King.

For weeks Hailey had looked forward to the holiday, imagining all the fun she'd have spending it with Winn and Cam. Now it looked as if it would be just her and Winn.

Winn was at the airport right now picking up Larry and Jan Robinette, who would spend the next three days reconnecting with their grandson. She'd wanted to ride along. Not only because she was curious and eager to meet them but to support Winn. Though he hid his concern well from

Cam, Hailey could see he was tense and worried about the visit.

"I thought you'd be hanging with Winn and grands tonight." Cassidy punctuated the comment by dumping a dustpan full of hair into the trash can.

"I wanted to," Hailey spun the chair to the right, then stopped and flung the chair in the other direction. "But Winn wouldn't budge. He absolutely refuses to do anything that might look like he's using me to gain leverage in a custody battle."

"Since when does Winn Ferris care what anyone thinks?"

"Exactly." Hailey grit her teeth and spun the chair hard. She looked up in surprise when it came to an abrupt halt.

"Stop with the spinning." Cassidy put a hand to her mass of blond hair tipped with royal blue. "You're making me dizzy. And more than a little crazy."

"You're always crazy." Hailey grinned up at her friend. "That's what I like about you."

"It's one of my most endearing qualities." Cassidy untied the leopard smock she'd worn over her purple tunic and black knit pants and whipped it off.

"You know what I like about you, chickadee." Cassidy dropped into the hot-pink salon chair next to Hailey's canary-yellow one, her vivid blue eyes surprisingly serious. "You've got spunk."

Hailey shook her head. Right now she felt more like a wimp than a warrior. "I'm not particularly...spunky."

Cassidy brought a long gold-tipped nail to her lips and continued as if Hailey hadn't spoken. "You remind me a lot of Sparky, the neighbor's terrier when I was growing up."

"What kind of terrier?" Hailey brightened. "A cute little Yorkie?"

"Rat terrier."

Hailey wrinkled her nose, not sure whether to laugh or be offended. "A *rat* terrier?"

"Don't make that face," Cassidy chided. "They're all heart and they don't back down."

"That's not me, Cass. I *do* back down."

Cassidy frowned. "That doesn't sound like my little rat terrier."

Hailey blew out an exasperated breath. "I wanted to be there to meet Cam's grandparents, but I let Winn make the decision."

"Why?" Cassidy didn't sound condemning of her or Winn, only curious.

"It's so darn important for him to show me he's not using me. He wants everyone in Jackson Hole to know I'm not a pawn in one of his schemes. I think he's supersensitive about that since our…disagreement last weekend."

"Winn Ferris. Supersensitive." A thoughtful look crossed Cassidy's face before she shook her head. "Not possible."

"Stop." With a laugh, Hailey reach out and swiped at her. "You're talking about the man I love."

And, dear God, how she loved him. Totally. Completely. With every fiber of her being. She loved him with a depth that would have been scary if it hadn't been so wonderful. The new level of trust between them had made it possible for her to let go of her fears and fully open her heart to him.

"I want to be Winn's wife, Cass. I want his face to be the last thing I see at night and the first thing I see when I wake up each morning. I want to be there for him day after day, year after year. I want to be Cam's mom. I want the three of us to be a family."

"Sounds like you know what you want, chickadee."

"I do." Hailey threw up her hands in frustration. "But Winn won't propose."

"There's one thing I remember best about Sparky." Cassidy's hot-pink lips lifted as she met Hailey's gaze. "If that dog saw something he wanted, nothing stopped him from getting it."

* * *

Independence Day turned out to be picture-perfect with temperatures in the low eighties and a sunny, cloudless sky. But what made it wonderful for Winn Ferris was that he was with the woman he loved.

Strolling with Hailey through Alpine Field, one hand holding hers, the other wrapped around a picnic basket, filled Winn with a contentment he'd never thought to find in this lifetime. The only thing that would make it more perfect was for Cam to be with them and for Hailey to be his wife.

Cole had said the past didn't determine the future. While that was true, his history of exploiting situations for his own gain had come to roost in the present. Winn vowed when he and Hailey started their married life together, no one would doubt his intentions were honorable and his love was true.

Still, he longed to put a ring on her finger, to publicly declare his love for her and his commitment to their future.

Hailey came to a halt in front of a massive bur oak. With a trunk diameter of at least eight feet, it soared toward the heavens. She smiled with satisfaction. "We have the best spot in the whole field."

This morning, while Cam had been chowing down on pancakes with his grandparents at the Jaycee Pancake Feed downtown, he and Hailey had participated in a land rush to stake their claim on this particular spot. The four stakes they'd laid out at nine were still there. The ribbons and flags they'd been issued in their surveyor's kit now fluttered in the light breeze.

The presymphony entertainment had just begun with a popular band belting out rock tunes. The Grand Teton Music Festival Orchestra wouldn't take the stage until six.

Still, the field buzzed with energy from the enthusiastic crowd. Local vendors had set up tents, providing food and beverages as well as games and activities.

Hailey spread the blue plaid blanket she'd carried draped over one arm on the ground, while Winn waited, holding a picnic basket filled with food and drink. Once she was satisfied with the placement, Hailey settled on the blanket and patted the spot beside her.

Winn took his place under the tree next to her. He glanced up at the leafy canopy shading them from the afternoon sun. "You were right. This is a perfect spot."

"If you get too close to the stage, it's loud and difficult to talk." Hailey smiled up at him, looking like an enchanting sprite with her hair pulled back in a flouncy tail. "It's a little farther to the concession stands from here, but we have our food and that fabulous bottle of wine. Plus, the tree makes it super easy for anyone to find us. So if Cam gets lonely—"

"He won't." Winn tried to sound cheerful. "Every time he sees Larry and Jan, he's excited. He's practically out the door before he remembers to say goodbye to me."

Cam had been glued to his grandparents' sides since he'd first seen them. At the airport, his son had run to their open arms, then, after lots of hugs and kisses, had tugged Larry and Jan back to him. Winn could tell they weren't too happy to hear Cam calling him Daddy.

To their credit, they didn't correct him and he could tell they were trying to be civil. He also had done his best to keep things pleasant.

Last night they'd had dinner together at Perfect Pizza. Winn had found himself wishing again for Hailey. She'd not only have charmed and put Larry and Jan at ease, she'd have steadied him.

"He loves you."

Winn blinked and focused on Hailey. She looked as sweet and delectable as an ice-cream sundae in her pink shorts and white top. But he'd learned there was a thread of steel behind the fluff. An intelligent woman who embraced the fun side of life but who had an inner strength to deal with whatever life would throw at her in the years ahead. Throw at *them,* he amended.

He couldn't wait to make her his wife. And he already knew she'd be a wonderful mother to Cam and to any other children they might have....

"I love you," he said suddenly, fiercely.

She lifted a hand, cupped his cheek and stared into his eyes. "I love you, too."

Just hearing the words brought a sweet relief to his heart and had the tension in his shoulders easing.

"We'll be together, forever," he promised. Placing his arms around her, he pulled her to him. His lips were on hers when his phone rang.

"Ignore it," she murmured.

"Can't." He sat back. "I gave my number to Larry and Jan in case of emergency."

Hailey kept her gaze on him as he pulled the phone from his pocket. Despite the heat of the day, a shiver went through her when his expression tensed.

"We're by the large oak," he said. "It's impossible to miss."

She expected him to hang up, but he continued to listen.

"It's no bother. This has been a lot for a little boy to handle." His expression softened and his voice sounded kind. "It'll give us a chance to become better acquainted. See you in five."

Worry formed a knot in Hailey's belly. "What happened?"

"Cam started crying, saying he wants me."

Though this should have been a moment of triumph for Winn, Hailey saw only concern for Cam in the worry furrowing his brow.

"They tried to soothe him but he insisted on seeing me. Apparently he's worried I left him."

Hailey took his hand, brought it to her lips for a kiss. "He's just a little boy who gets worried and scared."

"Hailey." Cam's voice rang out a second before he flung himself at her. "I didn't know you were here." He glanced around, his tear-streaked face bright and alert. "Is Bandit with you?"

She shook her head. "He's at home."

Cam turned back to his grandparents. "Bandit is a dog. He's Hailey's, but he likes me, too. I can show you all the tricks he can do."

"My goodness." Jan Robinette gave a laugh tinged with relief. She was a petite woman with tousled brown hair streaked with gray and kind eyes. "You've certainly perked up, little man."

"Yeah." Larry, a tall thin man with a thatch of wheat-colored hair, let out a breath. "By a thousand percent."

Cam hung his head and his smile faded. He shifted his gaze to his dad. "I thought you left me and wouldn't be back."

"That's not happening, sport." He pulled his son close and gazed over the boy's light brown hair to the Robinettes. "No way am I ever letting you go."

The warning in the words and the promise in his gaze was unmistakable.

Larry's eyes darkened. He opened his mouth to speak.

Before he had a chance, Hailey extended her hand and offered the couple a warm smile.

"I don't believe we've met. I'm Hailey Randall, Winn's fiancée."

Larry and Jan exchanged a quick significant glance. Beside her, she felt Winn still.

"Winn never mentioned that he was engaged."

"Can I see what's in the basket?" Cam asked.

"Certainly." Hailey tousled his hair, then, ignoring a stunned Winn at her side, refocused on the Robinettes.

"It's recent." Hailey let the abundance of love in her heart show in her eyes.

"I haven't had a chance to ask her father yet." Winn offered a rueful smile and played along. "Frank is a traditional guy, so I want to do everything by the book."

"Cam mentioned you like to fish." Hailey smiled at Larry. "My father has a couple of ponds on his property. I know my parents would love to meet you. If you're not busy tomorrow, we could all go fishing."

"Even me?" Cam looked up from the basket he'd begun unloading.

"Of course you," Hailey said.

"You could meet Bandit," Winn added. "Cam could show you his tricks."

"I—we'd—" Larry took his wife's hand "—like that."

"Grandpa had a snake in his house last time I was there." Cam spread his arms wide. "It was this big."

Jan turned white. "A snake?"

"Just a garter," Hailey said reassuringly. "They're not poisonous."

"Thank God." Jan paused and looked at Winn. "Grandpa? Your father?"

"No," Hailey answered quickly. No need to bring Jim Ferris into the mix. "My dad. Cam and he bonded almost instantly. My parents don't have any grandchildren yet, although my brother and his wife are expecting their first this spring."

"Brandon was our only child." Jan's eyes turned shiny with tears as she laid her hand on the boy's brown hair. "Cam is all we have."

"He loves you," Winn said in a soft voice so Cam wouldn't hear. "You love him. I was his father for six years before he was taken from my life. I know what it feels like to have someone you love snatched from you. I want you to still be involved."

"A child can't have too many people in his life who love him," Hailey added.

"Jackson Hole is just so far away," Jan murmured.

"Not that far," Winn said, seeming relieved when Tripp and Anna walked up.

Hailey performed the introductions, earning a curious look from Tripp when she introduced him as her brother, the mayor of Jackson Hole. The way she saw it, if anyone got to trade on her brother's status, it should be her.

Hailey sensed the pent-up tension in Winn. It didn't even dissipate when Tripp let him know the development was slated for approval.

It wasn't long until Tripp and Anna wandered off. Then Cam decided he wanted a snow cone. Larry and Jan left to take him to get one, promising to return shortly.

Neither Hailey nor Winn were worried, noticing the P.I. Winn had hired to monitor the couple's actions, standing at a discreet distance.

Winn cocked his head, staring at her. "You told them we were engaged."

She swallowed past the sudden dryness in her throat. "We are."

"When did this wonderful event occur?"

Despite his stern facade, the fact that he'd inserted the word *wonderful* gave her hope.

"The other night. When you told me you loved me and wanted us to be a family." She took his hand, twining her fingers through his. "I don't believe I gave you my answer. But I do want to marry you. I think it'd be a good idea for you to ask my dad for my hand tonight so he's not blind-sided tomorrow when the Robinettes start talking about our engagement."

"Our engagement."

"Yes. And don't worry about a ring. I'm okay with a simple wedding band."

"Well, I'm not." His gaze searched her eyes. "You deserve only the best."

"I've got the best," she stubbornly insisted.

Winn realized his instincts had been right—and all

wrong. Hailey believed in him, trusted in him, loved him. He'd been wrong to hold back for appearances' sake. To be sure, he'd done it with the best of intentions, but he hadn't fully taken into account the most important factor—what she wanted and needed from him.

Hailey's heart dropped as a second of silence turned into three.

"You say you're okay with a simple wedding band." Winn pulled a velvet box from his pocket, flipping it open revealing a chocolate oval diamond surrounded by even more glittering stones. "Are you saying you want me to take this back?"

"No. Ohmigosh. No." She stared down at the ring. When she lifted her gaze, tears swam in her eyes. "You said we had to wait."

"I meant we had to wait to make it official." He gave a self-conscious laugh. "I saw this in a window and it reminded me of you. I knew it was the one. Just like the stone, you're warm and down to earth yet full of vitality and life. There's a spark about you that comes through in everything you do."

"Just call me Sparky," Hailey said with a smile.

"Pardon?"

"Nothing. Tell me more. I like hearing how wonderful you think I am."

"I'm so lucky to have you in my life." He slipped the ring from the box and dropped to one knee, his eyes meeting hers. "I feel like I'm poised at the starting gate of the rest of my life. I'm ready—hell, I'm eager —to take on all the joys and sorrows, all the laughter and the pain, but only if you're by my side. I can't imagine making that journey without you. When I look into my heart, I see only you. I know my life will never be complete without you beside me to share it. Will you marry me? Will you be a wife to me and a mother to Cam?"

"I love you, Winn." Her voice shook with emotion. "No

one else will ever hold my heart the way you do. I would be proud to be your wife and a mother to Cam."

He slipped the ring on her finger then rose to kiss her long and hard.

"Now," he said with a smile, "we're engaged."

Epilogue

Less than two months later, on a warm September day, Hailey married Winn in a small ceremony on her parents' ranch. Under an arbor of flowers, they said their vows, surrounded by family and close friends.

Winn's father and grandfather were there. So far, Jim had been on his best behavior, complimenting his son on his choice of bride and not even flinching when Cam called him Grandpa.

Jan and Larry had flown in for the wedding and were staying at the ranch. Hailey's parents had gotten along so well with the Robinettes that they'd kept in touch. When Cam went to visit them over his school's fall break, Frank and Kathy would fly with him.

Winn's adoption of Cam was on track, only it would be both him *and* Hailey making Cam their forever son.

"Mrs. Ferris." Winn's lips lingered on the name as he twirled her on the dance floor. "How does it feel to be married to someone who's unemployed?"

She laughed. "I'm not sure my salary at the new clinic will be enough to keep you in the style to which you're accustomed, but I promise to do my best."

Tired of the antics of GPG, Winn had quit his job and was in the process of opening his own business, specializing in golf-course design and development. They both wanted to remain in Jackson Hole and although some travel would be required, Winn could do a lot of the design work from home.

"I'll work hard to make the business a success," Winn assured her. "But family will come first."

"Family and friends," Hailey said with a happy sigh, snuggling against him. "They're what makes a life complete."

"I didn't realize we'd invited Tim Duggan," Winn said, catching sight of the lanky physician on the edge of the dance floor.

"Cassidy asked me to invite him." Hailey slid her fingers through the back of Winn's hair, desire coursing through her like warm honey. She was ready for the honeymoon to begin.

"Why?"

Hailey wondered if it would be unseemly if she nibbled on her husband's ear.

"Why did she want you to invite him?" Winn repeated.

She pulled her attention from the lobe to her husband's handsome face. "I believe she's got the hots for him."

"Really?" Winn's expression was dubious. "I can't see them together."

"I can," Hailey said with a smile. "If anyone can make it happen it'll be Cass. She's got a boatload of terrier in her."

Winn opened his mouth then paused. "I'm not even going to ask what that means."

"Good. I've got something else in mind for your mouth than talking."

His gaze sharpened and heat flared in those beautiful hazel eyes. "Are you thinking what I'm thinking?"

Hailey grinned, a shiver of anticipation coursing up her spine. Not just for later tonight but for every night and day to come.

* * * * *

A sneaky peek at next month...

Cherish™

EXPERIENCE THE ULTIMATE RUSH OF FALLING IN LOVE

My wish list for next month's titles...

In stores from 18th July 2014:

❏ The Rebel and the Heiress – Michelle Douglas

& A Cowboy's Heart – Rebecca Winters

❏ Not Just a Convenient Marriage – Lucy Gordon

& The Billionaire's Nanny – Melissa McClone

In stores from 1st August 2014:

❏ A Wife for One Year – Brenda Harlen

& From Maverick to Daddy – Teresa Southwick

❏ A Groom Worth Waiting For – Sophie Pembroke

& Crown Prince, Pregnant Bride – Kate Hardy

Available at WHSmith, Tesco, Asda, Eason, Amazon and Apple

Just can't wait?

Visit us Online

You can buy our books online a month before they hit the shops! **www.millsandboon.co.uk**

0714/23

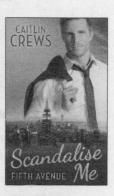

Discover more romance at

www.millsandboon.co.uk

- ❤ WIN great prizes in our exclusive competitions
- ❤ BUY new titles before they hit the shops
- ❤ BROWSE new books and REVIEW your favourites
- ❤ SAVE on new books with the Mills & Boon® Bookclub™
- ❤ DISCOVER new authors

PLUS, to chat about your favourite reads, get the latest news and find special offers:

- ⓕ Find us on facebook.com/millsandboon
- ⤷ Follow us on twitter.com/millsandboonuk
- ❤ Sign up to our newsletter at millsandboon.co.uk

The World of Mills & Boon

There's a Mills & Boon® series that's perfect for you. There are ten different series to choose from and new titles every month, so whether you're looking for glamorous seduction, Regency rakes, homespun heroes or sizzling erotica, we'll give you plenty of inspiration for your next read.

By Request

Relive the romance with the best of the best
12 stories every month

Cherish™

Experience the ultimate rush of falling in love.
12 new stories every month

INTRIGUE...

A seductive combination of danger and desire...
7 new stories every month

Desire™

Passionate and dramatic love stories
6 new stories every month

nocturne™

An exhilarating underworld of dark desires
3 new stories every month